LADY BLUESTOCKING'S FANCY

"I'm afraid you won't appreciate my saying it, but you are very lovely when you're angry." Southdon didn't know what was driving him to provoke her, but somehow he wanted to see Psyche turn into Lady Bluestocking before his own eyes. And she was magnificent, her eyes blazing, her chin thrust stubbornly out.

He liked the fierce way she glared at him. His Psyche was no milksop, no simpering maiden always bowing to his wishes. He smiled down at her. "I suppose I shall have to do this the conventional way. Would you honor me with this dance?"

"I—I . . . It is kind of you to ask me, but—"

He took a step closer. "Kindness has absolutely nothing to do with it," he replied with that lazy grin. "I *wish* to dance with you." He extended a hand.

Southdon looked so handsome at that moment that Psyche's heart began to thud painfully. "Very well," she said, trying not to smile in such a giddy fashion. "One dance."

A Memorable Collection of Regency Romances

BY ANTHEA MALCOLM AND VALERIE KING

THE COUNTERFEIT HEART   (3425, $3.95/$4.95)
by Anthea Malcolm

Nicola Crawford was hardly surprised when her cousin's betrothed disappeared on some mysterious quest. Anyone engaged to such an unromantic, but handsome man was bound to run off sooner or later. Nicola could never entrust her heart to such a conventional, but so deucedly handsome man. . . .

THE COURTING OF PHILIPPA   (2714, $3.95/$4.95)
by Anthea Malcolm

Miss Philippa was a very successful author of romantic novels. Thus she was chagrined to be snubbed by the handsome writer Henry Ashton whose own books she admired. And when she learned he considered love stories completely beneath his notice, she vowed to teach him a thing or two about the subject of love. . . .

THE WIDOW'S GAMBIT   (2357, $3.50/$4.50)
by Anthea Malcolm

The eldest of the orphaned Neville sisters needed a chaperone for a London season. So the ever-resourceful Livia added several years to her age, invented a deceased husband, and became the respectable Widow Royce. She was certain she'd never regret abandoning her girlhood until she met dashing Nicholas Warwick. . . .

A DARING WAGER   (2558, $3.95/$4.95)
by Valerie King

Ellie Dearborne's penchant for gaming had finally led her to ruin. It seemed like such a lark, wagering her devious cousin George that she would obtain the snuffboxes of three of society's most dashing peers in one month's time. She could easily succeed, too, were it not for that exasperating Lord Ravenworth. . . .

THE WILLFUL WIDOW   (3323, $3.95/$4.95)
by Valerie King

The lovely young widow, Mrs. Henrietta Harte, was not at all inclined to pursue the sort of romantic folly the persistent King Brandish had in mind. She had to concentrate on marrying off her penniless sisters and managing her spendthrift mama. Surely Mr. Brandish could fit in with her plans somehow . . .

Available wherever paperbacks are sold, or order direct from the Publisher. Send cover price plus 50¢ per copy for mailing and handling to Zebra Books, Dept. 3783, 475 Park Avenue South, New York, N.Y. 10016. Residents of New York and Tennessee must include sales tax. DO NOT SEND CASH. For a free Zebra/ Pinnacle catalog please write to the above address.

A Matchmaker's Match
Nina Porter

ZEBRA BOOKS
KENSINGTON PUBLISHING CORP.

for another Justin

ZEBRA BOOKS

are published by

Kensington Publishing Corp.
475 Park Avenue South
New York, NY 10016

First printing: June, 1992

Printed in the United States of America

Bluestocking: a learned or pedantic woman.

Chapter One

Lady Psyche Veringham pulled her favorite hunter up so violently that the poor beast snorted in dismay and almost threw her into the hedgerow, newly burst into bloom. She patted the gelding's smooth black neck in sympathy. "Easy, Hesperus, I'm sorry." Then she turned to frown at the man riding beside her, her cousin Viscount Overton.

"Really, Phillip. Now see what you've done? Hesperus will have a sore mouth tomorrow."

"The horse will survive," her cousin said, fussily smoothing his cravat. "Honestly, Psyche, you know if I had anyone else to ask I should do so. But Mama can't begin to manage a come-out. Not properly. And I want my ward to have the best."

"That is precisely my point," Psyche replied. "It's been years since my come-out. And I remember very little of it. Thank goodness."

Overton smiled sheepishly. "No matter. You've got to do a better job than Mama. Come, you know how Mama is."

Psyche did indeed. Overton's dear mama was just as empty-headed and giddy as her own dear departed mama had been. The Harley sisters had been cut from the same cloth, tonnish London said. And the town had never seen two such flibbertigibbets before or since.

Psyche frowned. It wasn't right to think poorly of the dead, but there was no way to avoid the painful truth. Mama had thought of nothing but fashion and titles. And that was where the trouble had started.

"Please, Psyche. Do this for me," Phillip pleaded, guiding his animal closer. "I don't know anything about managing a come-out."

There was no denying that. But a come-out meant a return to London. And London meant the trouble. Of course, it had been some years—five to be exact—since she had left the town. Perhaps the doings of Lady Bluestocking had been forgotten by now. After all, there were plenty of new *on-dits* to set fashionable tongues wagging.

And Phillip was her friend as well as her relation. She really did hate to turn him down.

"Tell me some more about her," she said, guiding the hunter around a puddle. "What's your ward's name?"

Overton smiled. "Her name's Amanda. Amanda Caldecott."

"And what sort of person is she?"

He looked puzzled. "I do not know."

Psyche raised an eyebrow. "You do not know? How can this be?"

He frowned, color flooding his cheeks. "Now,

8

Psyche, don't start bedeviling me. Amanda's a young thing, a mere chit, hardly out of the schoolroom. And I — You know I have been on the town for some years. My reputation — Well, you understand."

She resisted an impulse to laugh. "What has your reputation to do with anything?" she inquired sweetly.

He straightened in the saddle and gave her a hard look. "Why, I want Amanda to marry well. And, so as not to invite aspersions on her character, I kept her at the estate in Dover and only visited her twice a year."

Psyche shook her head. "Some would say you are remiss in your duty, cousin. But I think I understand."

Really, she thought Phillip's reputation as a man about town was much puffed, and mostly by himself, but there was no need to take the wind out of the man's sails by telling him so. It was rather amusing how these bucks put such value on their rakish reputations.

"So, tell me," she inquired, "what does your ward look like?"

"She's fair," Overton replied. "Shorter than you. Quite a little thing. With golden hair. Her eyes are blue and her figure trim."

"I see." Psyche grinned over at him. "I'm glad you've noticed her looks at least."

Overton smiled sheepishly. "Of course I have. And demned fine looks they are. But will you quit your teasing? Either fish or cut bait."

Psyche wrinkled her nose. "Really, Phillip, I

9

can't imagine your mama approving of such vulgar language."

Overton groaned in mock agony. "Must you keep mentioning Mama? Surely no man ever labored under a heavier burden."

Psyche sent him a commiserating look. "Speaking of burdens, how am *I* supposed to carry that of your mama?"

"You're a woman," he said, with a grin. "You know how to get around her."

"Ha!" Impatiently Psyche urged the hunter into a gallop. As Phillip well knew, people like his mama were impossible to get around.

Still, a short week later, there Psyche was, arriving at Tall Oaks, Phillip's estate in Dover. She had not promised definitely to undertake Amanda's come-out. She had agreed only to attend this house party and meet the girl.

As the servants began unloading her boxes, Phillip came hurrying down to greet her, closely followed by his mama.

Psyche blinked. The gown Aunt Anna was wearing defied human description. Constructed of some filmy gauzy material, it descended in wave after wave of fluttering yellow ruffles. Since Aunt Anna's complexion was on the sallow side and her figure of more than ample dimensions, the effect was far from pleasing — very far.

But Psyche had no time to contemplate her aunt's inadequate sense of fashion. Aunt Anna enveloped her in a hug that threatened to smother her in those very ruffles. And when her aunt released her, she smiled so sweetly that Psyche's heart sank. It was obvious that that cowardly Overton had neglected to tell his mother the real reason for her visit.

Psyche returned the smile. "Aunt Anna, how good to see you."

"We're so glad you could come," Aunt Anna trilled. "I haven't seen you for so long, child. Why, not since you lost your parents."

Psyche nodded. "Yes, Aunt." She hoped no one would refine on the carriage accident that had taken both her parents. Talking about it still hurt.

"Come," Overton said, taking her arm and leading her away from his mother who was already directing the servants. "I want you to meet Amanda."

Psyche looked around the pleasant garden, bright with spring blossoms. "Why didn't she come out here? It's such a lovely day."

Overton frowned. "She's too fair-skinned to be out in this sun." He glanced at Psyche's face. "And really, cousin, you should have a care for your complexion, too. With that dark hair and being so much in the sun — Why, you're so brown you could be taken for a Gypsy."

Psyche chuckled. "You did not malign my complexion last week when you came visiting me, cousin. Does this mean you have settled on someone else to manage the thing?"

"Good Lord, no!" He cast an anxious glance over his shoulder, pulling at his cravat. "Only don't tell Mama just yet. There's no need, till it's closer to the time."

11

Psyche patted his arm. "Poor boy. I know how it is. Remember, my mama was much like yours."

Overton frowned. "To think there were two of them. Truly, I don't see how you managed so well."

Psyche laughed, but it was a laugh without humor. "Oh yes," she said. "I managed so well that now I am a spinster."

Overton looked surprised. "I always thought that was by your choice."

Psyche shrugged. "I suppose in a way it was." She contrived a smile. "But take me to your Amanda. I have not come all this way to discuss my past foibles."

They entered the library through the French doors that led in from the garden. A slender girl came hurrying toward them, the ribbons on her white muslin gown fluttering. "Oh, milady—" She stopped, her mouth forming a pink oval of surprise.

"What is it, my dear?"

Amanda flushed. "I thought—That is, you are so terribly young."

Psyche chuckled, already finding the young woman to her liking. "I may be on the shelf," she said. "But I am not yet ancient."

"Oh dear," Amanda breathed, her fair face turning rosy. "I am in the suds now."

"Not at all," Psyche returned. "As you grow older you will learn that women never mind being told they look young."

Overton cast an anxious look over his shoulder. "I will go distract Mama so you two can get acquainted." And off he hurried.

"Well," said Psyche, taking off her bonnet and shaking her dark curls. "I suppose you know that my cousin has asked me to manage your come-out."

Amanda turned from looking after her guardian. "Oh yes, milady. And I pray you will do so. Lady Overton is—"

"She's a dear kind woman," Psyche said. "So was my Mama. Dealing with her was also difficult."

"You are so kind," Amanda said. "Not at all what I thought Lady Bluest—"

Psyche frowned. "You have heard the Lady Bluestocking stories?"

Amanda nodded. "Oh yes, milady. Many times."

Psyche sighed. "Then you must understand that if I decide to manage your come-out, the stories will most likely be revived."

Amanda nodded, blond curls bobbing emphatically. "But since we will be in London everyone will be able to see that you're not bracket-faced. They'll know—"

"Bracket-faced?" Psyche stiffened and looked around, grateful they were alone in the library. Of all the accusations made against her no one had ever before called her ugly. She was beginning to wish she'd stuck to her first sentiment and delivered a resounding—and final—no to Overton's request for help.

"Yes, milady. That's what I heard."

Psyche refrained from asking who had said such a thing of her. After all, she had not been in town for some years. And in the ton rumors were always quick to fly.

13

"Well," she said. "*If* I agree—and I only say if—you must be prepared for the gossips." She sighed. "In my day the worst of them was a mother-daughter pair—the Lindens."

Amanda's eyes grew round. "Oh yes! I have heard my guardian speak of them. Such horrible creatures!"

Psyche sighed. It looked like this was going to be no easy task. Amanda was a lovely girl, but did she have the understanding to make a really good match? Beauty was enough for some men, but a real tip-top Corinthian would expect to find a little more than an empty head behind that pretty face.

"Come," Psyche said, settling down on the settee. "Let us get acquainted."

They were still at it some minutes later when Psyche heard another carriage roll up outside. Amanda started to her feet, pulling nervously at the pink ribbons that decorated her gown. "Oh dear, someone else is arriving. And I know I shall appear addled. It's just that I do want to do my guardian justice. He has been so kind to me. And it is so important to him that I make a good match."

"And to you, too," said Psyche.

Amanda's eyes widened. "Yes, but I thought you disapproved of marriage."

Psyche frowned. Was she never to live down Lady Bluestocking's infamy? "We shall have to talk about that. You have been hearing some sorry tales about me, no doubt. But come, let's see who has arrived. Perhaps it's my friend, Georgette, Lady

Standish. I asked Overton to invite her."

Amanda moved toward the window. "No, it's not a lady. It's a gentleman!"

Curious, Psyche moved to look out the French doors. It was a gentleman, indeed, a fine figure of a man—his coat of blue superfine and his fawn inexpressibles bespeaking the work of London's finest tailors. His curly brimmed beaver had obviously come straight from the best hatter and his boots gleamed brilliantly in the sunlight.

Psyche found herself a little short of breath. It must be the prospect of being among people again. "Who is he?" she asked.

"The earl," Amanda breathed. "Justin St. James, Earl of Southdon."

He turned and Psyche saw a darkly handsome face—aristocratic nose, determined chin, and eyes . . . Her heart gave a peculiar little lurch in her chest.

"He's the one," Amanda continued. Her face aglow, she turned back to Psyche. "He's the man I'm going to marry."

"What! That is—" Aware of her proximity to the French doors, Psyche lowered her voice to a more reasonable tone. "Why him?"

"He's marvelous," Amanda breathed, her hands fluttering. "A tip-top Corinthian. The best catch of the Season."

"I see." She did not see at all. This child must have lost her mind. And Overton, too, to let her think of such a thing. "When did you meet the earl?"

Amanda smiled. "Oh, I have not met him, milady. I've only heard my guardian speak of him."

Psyche considered the innocent glowing face before her. Surely the girl had more understanding than that. "You mean to say that you intend to marry a man you have never even met?"

"Oh yes!" Amanda clasped her hands. "And, oh, milady, it is so kind of you to help me."

Chapter Two

As Psyche dressed for dinner she was of two minds. One mind demanded that she leave for home immediately. Let Aunt Anna manage — or mismanage — Amanda's come-out. Psyche didn't need a renewal of the trouble. And anyway, how could one manage a girl who thought she could snag the best catch of the Season — just like that!

But the other mind insisted, far too vehemently, that Overton had stood by her all these years. And that she had incurred a debt to her cousin for that very reason. Besides, no one — no matter how empty-headed — deserved a come-out managed by Aunt Anna.

So Psyche reserved judgment and put on her newest gown — a lovely creation of blush pink sarcenet trimmed with dark garnet ribbons. Surveying herself in the cheval glass, she felt her spirits lifting somewhat. She might be three and twenty and already on the shelf, but at least she didn't *look* old or spinsterish. There was a definite hint of color in her cheeks and a sparkle to her eyes.

17

Her dresser, threading garnet ribbons through the curls she had so artfully tumbled, sighed deeply. "This gown was a marvelous choice, milady. The pink do set off your dark hair."

"Thank you, Curtis. You have done an excellent job."

Psyche gave herself one long last look and nodded in satisfaction. Lady Bluestocking was ready to face the world. Or at least as much of it as was present there at Tall Oaks.

Moments later Psyche descended the stairs, her nerves well in hand. She would never have admitted it to anyone, of course, but she had been so long away from society that she was a trifle anxious about this house party. She squared her shoulders. If she meant to help Amanda to a proper marriage, she must get herself back into circulation, become accustomed to the banter and sport of the ton.

Overton met her at the door to the dining room. "Psyche, there you are. Do come meet our other guests."

He led her first to a short man with reddish hair and a round cheerful face. "The Viscount Gresham, my cousin Lady Psyche Veringham."

The viscount grinned. "May I say you look lovely tonight?"

Psyche nodded. "Of course. You may say it to every lady here." She smiled, at least her ability to trade repartee was still intact. "And no doubt you will."

The viscount chuckled and bowed.

"Here," Overton said, leading her on. "I want you to meet Southdon."

The earl turned and regarded her from jet black eyes.

"Southdon," Overton said. "My cousin, Lady Psyche Veringham."

One of the earl's black eyebrows lifted the merest smidgeon and the corner of his mouth inched upward. As he bowed, a strange breathlessness seemed to afflict her.

Bending low over her hand, the earl smiled to himself. She had long graceful fingers, just as he'd pictured them. He straightened. The rest of her was perfection, just as his mother had written to him.

He recalled the letters so well. He'd pored over them, there in the misery of Spain, till he could remember every word.

"She is tall and willowy," his mother had written. "With dark, dark curls and eyes like deep purple pansies. Her nose is perhaps a little too aristocratic, her chin a little too determined for a woman. But she's a beauty, a real beauty."

He had treasured those words and every scrap of information his mother had sent him about the daring and legendary exploits of Lady Bluestocking, treasured them and imagined *her*. In a very real sense Lady Bluestocking had kept him alive through a long and difficult campaign.

And so at last he'd come home, to search for her, the darling of his heart. And now she was standing in front of him, in the flesh, the beautiful flesh.

But Lady Bluestocking hated men, his mother had written. Lady Bluestocking wanted nothing to do with marriage. Still, he was not going to let that stop him. His mother had posited that Lady Bluestocking had hated the individual men presented to her, not marriage to one she loved. And that was what he had come to believe.

She had been wounded, his beautiful, feisty Lady Bluestocking, by her overzealous and title-conscious maternal parent, but she could be healed. And he was the man to do it.

Psyche, returning the earl's gaze, felt the color rush to her cheeks. He regarded her so steadily, as though he were looking for something in her face. And then it struck her that the earl knew. He knew she was Lady Bluestocking. She'd been foolish to think the old stories would be forgotten. Gossip-mongers were always ready to spread tales, new or old.

Overton dropped her arm. "I'll be back in a minute," he said. "Mama is calling me."

And, indeed, across the room Aunt Anna, a mountainous figure in a waterfall of mauve ruffles, was urgently waving a huge gilt fan.

Left alone with the earl, Psyche tried to think of some way to move off, but her slippers seemed stuck to the floor. "Have you known Overton long?" she asked finally.

The earl nodded. "We were at Harrow together. He was below me, of course."

"Of course." For the life of her she could think of nothing more to say. All her social skills seemed to have deserted her.

The earl regarded her seriously. "Overton tells me he's asked you to manage his ward's come-out."

20

Trust Overton to blab the thing about. He should have kept quiet till he had heard her decision. Psyche glanced toward Aunt Anna. "Yes. But I have not yet agreed."

The earl smiled and for some strange reason the room seemed suddenly brighter. "I think you should do it," he said.

Surprise made her stare at him. "You do? But why?"

He took her gloved hand in his. "If I may—"

Slightly shocked but fascinated, she nodded assent. "First," he touched her index finger with his, "you can obviously do a better job than—That is, it takes a younger—"

She chuckled. "There's no need to skirt the obvious. We all know Aunt Anna does not manage well."

He smiled again. "Lovingly put. So you must step into the breach."

"Perhaps."

"And second," he touched another finger, "and more importantly, London should not be denied your presence."

The compliment took her quite by surprise; it was done so skillfully. She mustered her defenses, terribly conscious that her hand still rested in his, and that she was reluctant to withdraw it. "You're very kind, milord. But there are definite disadvantages to my undertaking the task."

His eyes grew warm—oh, he was a master at this kind of verbal repartee. "Strange," he said, his voice dropping an octave, "I cannot think of a single one."

She forced herself to frown. "You forget who I am."

He shrugged. "You are Lady Psyche Veringham."

She gave a little gasp—he had pronounced her name the Greek way—*See kay*. No one but Papa had ever done that.

"You know classic Greek?" she asked.

He nodded, the end of his mouth curling up again. "Oh yes, a little. And I know your name means 'soul.' I am much interested in antiquities, you see."

"Indeed." She was hard put to understand why this news should set her heart to racing. Or perhaps that was because he was still holding her hand. Regretfully, she withdrew it.

"So," he went on, "you have not told me why you are unfit for this task."

"I am—" But perhaps he didn't know. She hesitated, reluctant to face the old trouble.

"You are Lady Bluestocking," he said cheerfully. "I know that. Though I was in Spain at the time of your escapades, I heard all the tales."

"So you must see—"

He shrugged, his expression nonchalant. "Surely there is no scandal in refusing to wed. The world knows you could have had offers enough." His eyes narrowed. "And yet you took none of them. I wonder why."

She did not consider evading his question. "The thing was—I wished to marry for love."

"And?" His eyes seemed to bore into her very heart.

22

"And I did not find it."

"I see." He stroked his chin thoughtfully. "A pity, that. A lovely woman like you."

Psyche smiled. "Really, milord, your style of compliment is excellent. But aren't you doing it up rather brown?"

He sighed in exaggerated fashion. "Alas, they were right. They told me you had a wicked sharp tongue."

She couldn't help herself, she had to ask him. "Who? Who told you that?"

He grinned, looking suddenly much younger, and even more attractive than he had before. "Why, the Lindens, of course. The inestimable and excessively ample Lady Linden and her stickish daughter." He frowned. "They have already revived stories of every Lady Bluestocking escapade — and probably added a few of their own devising."

She regarded him seriously. "And yet you urge me to return to that?"

The earl shrugged, a gesture that automatically took her gaze to the breadth of his shoulders. "Yes," he said dryly. "I urge you to return to town and live down this Linden-induced infamy."

Psyche had to return to London, otherwise how would he be able to win her? He wished he could ask her then. But he would have to go slow. In a sense, she had fought her wars, too. With her addlepated mama pressing foppish witlings or doddering old lords on her just because they had titles. And with the tattle-bearing Lindens and their ever-present innuendoes making her life unbearable.

Yes, Lady Bluestocking had her wounds, but

they would heal. He would see to it.

Overton, of course, didn't know that the idea of Psyche managing his ward's come-out had *not* been his own, but had been planted in his mind by his good friend, the earl. Overton knew nothing of the earl's fascination, infatuation, captivation with the fabled Lady Bluestocking. Only Georgie knew that. And Georgie had promised not to tell, but to help.

"You *can* face the Lindens," he said, giving Psyche an admiring gaze.

Psyche frowned. How could the man be so sure? "I don't know. I have been long in the country."

He shrugged. "I have confidence in you."

Psyche flushed. "Is it true they have called me bracket-faced?" This man was having the strangest effect on her. What a ridiculous question to ask! After all, vanity was not for spinsters.

The earl coughed delicately. "I'm afraid it's true." His gaze met hers, his eyes full of laughter. "They have quite departed from the truth in saying it, of course. As any fool could see." He smiled. "But after the last set-down you gave me I dare not offer another compli—"

"Psyche!" Georgette rushed between them to envelope Psyche in a hug. "How good to see you!" When she withdrew and settled her gown, Georgie was smiling. "I see you have met Southdon. Be careful of him. He's got quite a name with the ladies."

Psyche managed to go on smiling. Not for the world would she have admitted wishing that she hadn't suggested to Overton that he invite Georgie

24

to this house party. Dearly as she loved her, Georgie could be a trifle overwhelming — and sometimes she was far from sensible. But she was also extremely attractive to men.

Georgie was the little petite sort and her recent widowhood had hardly dampened her perennial good spirits. Of course, her dear departed husband had been some forty years her senior. And now Georgie, who had married first to please her family, meant to marry second to please herself. Or so her letters had proclaimed.

"Dear Georgie," Psyche murmured. "How good to see you. I have found the earl a most fascinating conversationalist."

His eyes twinkled and he grinned brashly. "But can you imagine, Lady Standish, Lady Psyche does not relish my style of compliment?"

Georgie actually giggled and put her gloved hand familiarly on the earl's coat sleeve. "Poor Psyche's been too long in the country," she said. "But come, Southdon. You may compliment *me*." And she thrust her arm through his and led him off.

Watching them go, Psyche struggled with the urge to turn tail and run. Little Amanda was right. Southdon *was* the catch of the Season. And that meant Overton's ward was going to face some brisk competition.

Of course, Georgie had always enjoyed the company of men. In fact, her youthful reputation had marked her as rather fast. But she had listened to her family — married where they chose. The first time. Now she was a widow and able to do as she pleased.

Perhaps, Psyche couldn't help thinking, perhaps *she* should have done the same. Though she was financially as well off as Georgie, she was still Lady Bluestocking, still the subject of gossip. And still a spinster. It hardly seemed fair.

But Psyche had never been one to feel sorry for herself. She had chosen to be Lady Bluestocking. And in its time the role had served her well. It had saved her from marriage to more than one foppish fribble, and several men old enough to be her grandfather. She could thank Papa for Lady Bluestocking. It was, after all, his study of antiquities that had given her the idea.

"Why so serious?" the earl inquired, appearing at her side again. "Surely the decision is not that difficult to make."

Psyche looked at him in surprise. "Where is Georgie?"

He smiled. "I believe Lady Standish is talking to Gresham over there. And I have come back to reiterate my plea that you consent to manage Miss Caldecott's come-out."

He glanced across the room to where a radiant Amanda stood talking to several people. "The girl's a good sort and deserves a decent chance." He smiled. "Besides, Overton's my friend. He's a decent chap, too. And he's really been in a twitter over this."

Psyche nodded. "Yes, I know. Do—" She hesitated, but then decided to plunge ahead. "Tell me, Southdon, what sort of man do you think Amanda should marry?"

He looked a little surprised, but he stroked his

chin again. "Someone older, I suppose. Someone who's been on the town for a while and is ready to settle down. To take care of her."

Psyche nodded. "Yes, I suppose she will need taking care of."

His eyes were so dark, they seemed to be hiding some secret. "Not all women are as well equipped as Lady Bluestocking for the unmarried life," he remarked.

She schooled her face, hoping to keep her expression from betraying her. If the man only knew the nights she'd cried herself to sleep, wondering if she should have accepted one of Mama's awful candidates. But there had been no one she could . . .

She drew herself up. "I suppose a woman may go through life alone as well as any man." She fixed him with a stern eye. "You, milord, for instance, you are yet unwed, but that does not seem to concern you."

He raised an eyebrow. "Concern? No, I should say not. In fact, it makes me quite happy. But I shall have to marry—eventually. My mother is adamant on that point."

Psyche swallowed a little sigh. "She probably wishes to have grandchildren."

The earl grinned. "So she tells me, repeatedly. I do not know why women find children so attractive." His eyes gleamed with merriment. "It seems to me that they incite a great deal of anxiety."

After a delightful dinner, which Psyche spent in conversation with the earl regarding the Elgin Marbles, she retired with the other ladies to the drawing room.

Before she could even settle into a chair, Amanda appeared at her side. "Well, what do you think?"

Psyche saw Georgie's inquisitive look. "Not now, Amanda. We'll talk later."

But Amanda would not be put off. She grabbed Psyche by the arm. "Oh, milady, I must know now! Aren't you agreed? Don't you think the earl would make me a wonderful husband?"

Georgie's small gasp wasn't lost on Psyche. She felt a rising irritation. If Amanda was going to act this bird-witted, she'd have little chance of success.

She took the young woman by the arm. "Excuse us, Georgie."

Georgie nodded, but she looked ready to burst with curiosity.

Psyche led Amanda to a secluded corner where she looked at her sternly. "Amanda, when I say *not now,* I mean *not now.* If you expect to win a husband, you must learn discretion."

Amanda looked surprised, her blue eyes widening in shock, her pink mouth forming an oval of dismay.

"Suppose," Psyche continued, "that Lady Standish were to tell the earl what you just said."

Amanda's eyes grew even rounder. "She wouldn't! She's your friend."

Psyche knew better. Friend or no, if Georgie wanted the earl, she would go after him. And she would use any available means to get him. She sighed. "Amanda, have you never heard the expression—'All's fair in love and war?'"

Chapter Three

The next morning Psyche rose early, put on her claret-colored riding habit, and made her way to the stable. Morning air always cleared her mind and this morning it felt in particular need of clearing.

The events of the previous evening were foremost in her mind as she turned Hesperus away from Tall Oaks. The gelding tossed his handsome head: it was obvious he wanted a good run.

"Not now," she told him. "We don't know this country well enough."

She held the horse to a walk, but her mind was not so easily controlled. It insisted on galloping over the events of the night before. Imagine meeting someone like the earl now. If she had met him before, during her Season, there might not have been any need to create Lady Bluestocking.

But he hadn't been in London then; he'd been off fighting Napoleon. And so her Season had come — and gone, leaving her unwed.

Oh, even the second year she might have accepted several offers. But she had continued to play Lady Bluestocking to the hilt and so frightened her suitors that they'd cut and run. She'd had to do it — marriage to any of them would have meant disaster. She'd known it then, and she knew it now.

Hesperus had halted. Looking up, she saw that he stood outside the wall of a ruin. From the lay of it, it could be what was left of an abbey. She couldn't be sure.

In any event there was a quiet grace about the place. Tendrils of ivy crept over the tumbled stone, harbingers of spring, opening green buds to the sun.

Psyche sighed. Just a few weeks remained to prepare for the Season. But could she undertake such a task? Did she want to go back into the world of the ton? They were not kindhearted, those people who fed on gossip, who lived for the *on-dit,* the whispered scandal, the ruined reputation.

She might not be considered bracket-faced yet, but she had to admit she *was* on the shelf. There was no skirting the fact that she was three and twenty, long past the prime age for marriage. And worse, her reputation as Lady Bluestocking had not been buried. Or, more accurately, it had been resurrected by the Lindens.

"I had to do it," she said, scratching behind the gelding's ears. "I had to protect myself from those creatures Mama pushed on me. I had to create Lady Bluestocking."

The horse snorted and tossed his mane. "I know," she said. "You want a nice run. But I don't. Not yet at least." She gazed around. "I believe I'll just take a look at these ruins. Perhaps the abbey was built on the remains of something Roman."

She slid down and tethered the horse to a tree. The stones were all tumbled about, but in the far corner part of a wall had survived intact. A lot could be surmised by looking at the stones themselves. Papa had taught her that chisel marks often had a tale of their own to tell.

She set out for the corner, picking her way carefully among the scattered stones. The way was rough, the ground uneven. Holding up her riding skirt, she stepped cautiously. She thought she was being quite careful, yet one minute she was upright and walking, and the next her ankle had turned and she was thrown violently to the ground.

"Oh!" Her Cossack-styled riding hat kept her head from hitting directly on the stones. And her heavy velvet habit protected her skin from scrapes, but her entire body felt jarred by the fall. Tomorrow would bring a fair-sized bruise on her derriere. There was no doubt in her mind of that.

She started to push herself upright. Pain jolted through her and she cried out. Her foot was trapped under a heavy block of building stone. Evidently the weight of her stepping on it had tilted the stone sideways and when she fell it flipped over on top of her foot.

After she caught her breath, she tried again to reach it. But the stone was too big and heavy, and her foot was twisted at an angle that made it hard to get at.

She sank back with a sigh, frustrated. It was clear that she could not free herself. Forcing herself into calmness, she tried to settle comfortably. Though her foot was trapped, it was not excessively painful. She would just be in for a longish wait. Since it was yet early morning, no one would be apt to miss her for some time.

There was little point in ranting and railing at her fate, however. She was pinned there till someone found her — no amount of complaining would change that.

Well, she had wanted to be alone, to clear her head so she could decide whether or not to help Amanda. And here she was — certainly alone. With plenty of morning air and plenty of time to think.

She gave herself up to considering the pros and cons of returning to London. At the end of the first hour she had come no nearer a conclusion. What she had concluded was that the stones were quite hard and that she could find no comfortable position among them. For the first time her courage faltered a little. No one at the house knew where she had gone, not even what direction. How would they know where to look for her?

The sun came out from behind a cloud, forcing her to close her eyes against its glare. Perhaps she would doze a little. The time would pass faster.

The earl pushed his horse harder. Why hadn't he risen earlier? He hadn't expected Psyche to go out riding alone. He'd meant to be there before her, to suggest he ride with her.

But he had laid awake long into the night, recalling her every word, her every look. So that this morning he'd been late to rise, too late to catch Psyche.

Besotted, he told himself, *you're absolutely besotted with the woman.* But he didn't care. He only hoped he could find her. The stable boy had said there were ruins in this direction—and he was hoping that she had decided to ride there.

And then he saw them, great blocks of tumbled stone, probably once an abbey. Seconds later he spied the horse, its saddle empty. Was Psyche examining the ruin? But where?

And then the splotch of claret caught his eye, claret among the gray stones of the ruin. She was on the ground!

He pulled the horse to a halt, dismounted, and hurried to her. "Psyche?"

She didn't stir. She looked to be asleep, but with that building stone on her foot she could be injured. If she'd fallen and hit her head—

He moved closer, repeating her name, this time a little louder. "Psyche! Are you hurt?"

She stirred then and opened her eyes. He let out his breath in relief. "Well," he said, making his tone jocular, "what have we here?"

Psyche jerked awake and looked up to see the Earl of Southdon looming over her. "Southdon, are you really here?"

He smiled. "To the best of my knowledge. But what—"

"I slipped and my foot got caught." She flushed. "I know it was foolish. Papa would have scolded me. He always cautioned me against clambering about ruins alone."

33

"A wise man," the earl observed, moving closer. "Let me get this stone off your foot." He lifted it easily and set it to one side.

Psyche sighed. "Thank you. That feels much better."

He tested her ankle, his fingers gentle. "We really should get that boot off. In case your foot swells."

"Yes, I suppose so."

He straddled her legs, his broad back to her. "Can you brace yourself with your other foot?"

"I—" To do what he suggested she would have to plant her other foot directly on the seat of his immaculate inexpressibles.

He glanced back over his shoulder. "What are you waiting for?"

The blood rushed to her face. "I—Your—"

"Just put your boot where it will do the most good." He grinned. "And count yourself fortunate. Few people get such an opportunity."

She decided to take him at his word and set her good foot firmly on the seat of his breeches. "Ready."

"All right. I'm going to make it quick. It'll probably cause you some pain, but to go slow would only drag it out."

She nodded. What sort did he think she was? Lady Bluestocking would not cry out. That kind of carrying on was for frailer females. She braced herself against the rocks. "I'm ready."

True to his word, he was quick. The boot came off with a jerk and she fell back among the stones, not quite able to contain a little whimper.

He turned to her at once, his eyes full of concern. "I'm dreadfully sorry, but leaving your boot on would have made it much worse. And cutting one off can be tricky business."

She moistened her dry lips. "I — I am fine. Thank you for your help."

To prove she was fine she started to get up, to show him she could do so quite easily, but the world, unfortunately, refused to stand still. Indeed, it commenced spinning in dizzying circles and then, quite to her astonishment, the ground came rushing up to meet her.

In that last second before the darkness hit she felt the earl's strong arms closing around her. She was conscious of the smell of leather and his pomade. And then there was nothing.

She opened her eyes to find herself lying in his arms. For the briefest second she fought the temptation to close her eyes again, to savor the moment.

He frowned in concern. "Lady Psyche, are you in much pain?"

"I —" She struggled to sit erect, terribly conscious of his arms around her. "I am not in pain." She frowned. "Well, perhaps just a little. But I am frightfully dizzy. The result of my fall, no doubt." She hesitated. "Perhaps you could help me to my horse?"

He raised a dark eyebrow. "And have you fall off him into my arms? I think not. You might injure yourself further."

"But . . ." Actually the prospect of falling into his arms did not seem at all daunting. Why must the man have such a bewitching smile?

"No buts," he continued. "I would be remiss in

my duty if I allowed such a thing."

She looked at him in bewilderment. "But then how shall I get back to the house?"

He gazed directly into her eyes. "You must ride with me, of course."

Her heart began to pound in mad confusion. "With you?"

"Yes." His smile was tender. "I shall lift you into the saddle first, then swing up behind you. But you must call out immediately if you feel faint. Do you understand?"

"Yes, but . . ."

"Good. I shall carry you out to the horses then and we'll be on our way."

"There's no need to carry me," she protested. "I mean, I can lean on your arm."

"Perhaps," he said. "But I prefer not to take that risk."

"I am not a small woman," Psyche began, painfully aware of the impropriety of being carried. And by such a man, by a man who already made her heart pound in a dreadful fashion.

The earl shrugged. "I'm much larger, and I'm no weakling." Moments later he was on his feet and lifting her into his arms.

She discovered that she was quite comfortable there, in his arms. He had a strength to him, imparting a certain sense of safety to her. But she was conscious, too, of some other feelings, feelings that might prove quite dangerous.

Picking his way carefully among the scattered stones, the earl was soon back to where the horses waited.

He set her on her good foot first, keeping his hands on her waist, his face so close to hers that she could feel his warm breath. Then he lifted her right up onto the saddle.

"Hang on while I get your boot," he said with a worried look. "Don't faint on me now."

"I'm fine." She was feeling light-headed again, actually rather giddy. But she strongly suspected the feeling was caused by the earl and not the pain in her ankle which only throbbed a little.

He came back with her boot and tucked it under a strap on her saddle. Then he loosened the horses, holding both sets of reins, and swung up behind her. It was a strange sensation, having a man so close. One she liked. The men who had pursued Lady Bluestocking had been the sort a woman wanted to get away from, not get close to.

She tried to sit erect. This was, after all, the man Amanda loved. If she meant to help the girl, she could not give in to these feelings of weakness that threatened to engulf her. And at any rate the earl was only being kind. Last night's repartee was only that — witty badinage to pass the time. He knew she was Lady Bluestocking, and therefore not interested in matrimony.

Nevertheless, she felt a terrible inclination to melt back against him. She stiffened her spine. Perhaps conversation would help to distract her. "How did you happen to be out here?" she asked.

His arms were so strong around her, gathering her closer. But she shouldn't think of that. Or the feel of his chest against her back, his warm masculine chest.

"I just thought I would explore the ruins," he said. "Remember, I am interested in antiquities."

She smiled. "How fortunate for me. I might have lain there for a long time, undiscovered."

"Yes." His voice was rough. "You really should tell the stable boy where you're heading when you ride out."

"How do you know I didn't?"

"Because I asked him."

The answer was obvious, but still it startled her. "Oh."

"I saw your hunter was gone and so I asked." His voice grew stern. "You really should not put yourself in such danger."

"You needn't read me a scold," she said. "I did not mean to injure my foot. It was an accident."

"*I* know that."

She twisted, trying to see his face. "Why do you say that in such a strange tone?"

He smiled grimly. "I have been on the town for some years. And during that time I have had numerous young ladies fall into my arms. Down the stairs, from carriage steps, and from just about any place else you might think of." He sighed. "Unfortunately, many young women seem prone to falling when they are within reach of my arms."

"You don't say." Psyche straightened again. The man certainly had a good opinion of himself. "Well, thank goodness you were not present when I fell and *I* can be spared such an accusation."

His arm tightened around her, pulling her back against his chest again. "Don't get your hackles up now. I'm only stating facts. You can't suppose that

I enjoyed it. Any more than you enjoyed the kind of suitors your maternal parent chose for you."

The earl felt the slight stiffening of her body as it leaned against his. *Fool!* he told himself. *It's too soon to let her know what you've guessed.*

He kept his mouth shut and concentrated on holding her close, tenderly. He'd never expected to have her in his arms so soon. The experience had almost unnerved him, left him so weak in the knees he hadn't been sure he could carry her. But he'd managed and here she was, tucked up in front of him on the saddle.

And he was allowed — not constrained — to put his arm around her lovely waist, to inhale the sweet scent of her hair. *Careful,* he told himself. *She's skittish still. Give her time, don't scare her.*

"You don't need to converse," he told her quietly. "Just lean against me."

Psyche really tried to remain erect, but in such proximity to the earl, she was utterly incapable of it. And so she spent the next miles melting backward into his waistcoat.

They reached the stable far too soon to suit her. Why couldn't they have gone on riding forever?

The stable boy came hurrying up.

"It's all right," the earl said. "The lady just twisted her ankle."

The stable boy nodded and took the horses. The earl slid down and raised his arms to her.

"I can — " she began, but he did not wait to hear her finish. His hands closed around her waist and he lifted her down. She felt the giddiness returning and reached out to him. "I — "

"Easy now." He gathered her into his arms and turned to the waiting stable boy. "You'll find her boot tied to her saddle. See that it's sent up to the house."

"Yes, milord."

The earl started off toward the house, striding easily. "Really," Psyche said, looking up at him, so handsome, so near. "I'm sure I could walk if you would just allow me to lean on your arm a little."

His dark face, so close to her own, twisted into a frown. "Indeed, I will not. I intend to carry you and that is that."

Psyche sighed. "Very well. But kindly bear in mind that this was all your idea."

"Of course it was. I should certainly never be ungentlemanly enough to chide a lady over her carelessness."

"Carelessness!" she cried. "You have bats in your attic. I was not careless. I am never careless. I could hardly be expected to know—"

Something in his expression alerted her and she stopped in midsentence, looking around to discover that they had just crossed through the French doors into the library. And they were not alone.

Around them stood the assembled guests, staring with unconcealed curiosity at the spectacle before them. Psyche felt the blood rushing to her cheeks.

And then from the doorway came a voice she had hoped never to hear again. Miss Linden trilled, "Why, Lady Psyche, what could *you* possibly not know?"

40

Chapter Four

An hour later Psyche was settled in her chamber. Knowing that it was well meant, she had stoically endured Aunt Anna's fluttering and fuming. But she found herself most grateful when the physician arrived and Aunt Anna departed, sent to her bed with an order to rest her nerves.

Then the physician said Psyche had a bad sprain and suggested she stay off her foot.

Finally only her cousin remained, nervously pulling at his cravat. "Are you quite sure you're all right?" he asked anxiously.

"Quite sure," Psyche replied, "except for one thing."

"And what is that?"

She glared at him. "Overton, why on earth did you invite *them* here?"

He avoided her gaze. "Invite whom?"

"You know perfectly well who I mean—those awful Lindens."

He frowned. "But I didn't invite them. They came knocking on the door this morning. Said

they were traveling and Lady Linden took sick."
He pulled at his cravat again. "What was I to do,
Psyche? After Mama asked them in I couldn't
turn them away."

Psyche sighed. "Perhaps not. But mark my
words—those two mean trouble."

Shortly before the dinner hour someone rapped
on Psyche's door. "Come in," she called eagerly.
After a long and wearisome afternoon of doing
nothing she would welcome almost any visitor.

She smiled. "Georgie! Do come in."

The small slender sort, Georgie, looked good in
anything, but this deceptively simple gown in the
Grecian style had no doubt cost her late husband
a pretty penny. Its Bishop's blue had clearly been
chosen to go with her eyes, but it was her gamine
smile that made her most attractive. Psyche motioned her toward the bed. "You look marvelous."

Georgie grinned. "Don't I, though? It's the
most wonderful thing. When I got out of mourn-
ing, I ordered all the gowns I wished and there
was no Standish to read me a lecture." She col-
ored a little. "Not that I ever wished him ill."

"I know." Psyche smiled at her friend. Georgie
was a little on the flighty side, and she probably
wasn't above an occasional innocent flirtation,
but she was basically a good person.

"So," she said, perching on the edge of the
great bed. "How is your injured ankle?"

42

"It throbs a little," Psyche admitted. "But the surgeon said it will not swell much."

To her surprise, Georgie giggled. "No, I don't suppose it will. Come, tell me now, how did you get the stone on top of it? Did you see him coming and then do it?"

"Of course not." Psyche frowned. Trust Georgie to make something complicated of the simplest accident. "I stepped on a stone wrong and it flipped over and pinned my foot. I was trapped for some time before Southdon arrived."

Georgie nodded, but her eyes danced with merriment. "Whatever you say, my dear. But I wish I'd thought of it. It's much better than falling from the top step or — Psyche, stop it, why are you laughing at me like that?"

Psyche swallowed hastily. "I'm not laughing at *you*. He told me — You mean he was right? Young women do actually fall into his arms?"

"Of course they do." Georgie patted her hand. "My dear, this man is the catch of the decade. Every young woman in the ton hopes to bag him. And some older ones, too."

Psyche sighed. "And Amanda had to set her sights on him."

Georgie shook her head. "The girl's being foolish. Southdon is not for her. He likes his women older." She smiled slyly. "And with experience."

While Psyche considered this, Georgie stared at her. "Are you really going to do it?"

"I don't know." Belatedly Psyche remembered that Aunt Anna as yet knew nothing of her niece's part in the come-out. "Do what?"

"No need to hedge," Georgie said, raising an eyebrow. "Overton told me he asked you to manage his ward's come-out." She frowned, smoothing her silken skirt. "She's pretty enough. But she's not for Southdon."

"I don't suppose *we* can decide that," Psyche said, uncomfortably aware that she wished to agree with her friend, wished it very much. "That's up to him."

"True enough." Georgie got to her feet. "But you haven't answered my question. Are you going to do it?"

"I don't know."

Georgie nodded. "The Lindens are saying you won't, that you don't dare come back to town." She frowned and patted her hair. "They seem to think they are responsible for your leaving."

"What!" Psyche reared up. "This is the outside of enough! First they call me bracket-faced and—"

Georgie raised a hand to her mouth. "Psyche, they didn't!"

"Oh yes they did! It's time someone put those two—two backbiters—in their place."

"And you're just the one to do it," Georgie added, turning toward the door. "Overton will be pleased."

"Georgie! I didn't say—"

"Rest now," Georgie said, with a smug smile Psyche found annoying in the extreme. "You'll need your strength."

And then she was gone. Psyche glared at the

curtains that surrounded the great bed. The Lindens were a scourge, a pair of scandalmongers par excellence. But she would not let them drive her home again, like a fox into a bolt-hole.

She swung her legs around to the edge of the bed. Enough of this resting. But just as her good foot touched the floor, the door burst open.

"I'm sorry, milady," Amanda cried, rushing in, her gown fluttering, her curls bouncing. "But I can't wait any longer. I must talk to you now."

Psyche swallowed a sigh. This was not the sort of company she'd been thinking of, but she schooled herself to patience and leaned back among the pillows. "Yes, Amanda. What is it?"

Amanda made a moue of disgust. "The Lindens are saying the most horrid things about you. Miss Linden has a most wicked—"

"What kind of horrid things?" Psyche asked wearily. It looked like she was in for more discomfort from the Lindens, a lot more.

Amanda wrung her hands—a vapid gesture obviously learned from Aunt Anna. "They are saying that you don't mean to help me with my come-out at all. That—That you are angling for the earl yourself." She eyed Psyche tearfully. "They said—They said you hurt your foot on purpose. That it was all a ruse."

This time Psyche didn't manage to swallow her sigh. "The Lindens are wrong," she said. "I am not trying to snare the earl. And I did not trap my ankle under a building stone on purpose." To think that the chit would be taken in like that!

45

"But you may believe them if you like. I'm sure Aunt Anna will be more than glad to help you with your come-out."

Amanda paled, obviously distressed at the prospect. "Oh no! I don't—I won't believe them. Please, please, milady, say you'll help me!"

Psyche surrendered to the inevitable. She had never been able to forego a challenge. And certainly the Lindens had issued one. "Very well," she said. "I will do it. But you must not tell the Lindens I have agreed. Not just yet."

Amanda smiled through her tears. "Oh, I shan't! How very kind you are. Oh, I do hope your sprain is soon healed."

"Thank you, Amanda. You'd better run along now and get dressed for dinner."

"Of course. And—And thank you again."

Amanda went hurrying out and Psyche moved to swing her feet over the bed.

"Here, here. What are we doing?" the earl asked, appearing in the doorway.

"We," she replied, shooting him a dark look, "are getting up."

He looked dubious. "Is that wise? After all, your sprain—Doctor Higham said you must stay off your foot."

"Did he also say that I must be consumed by boredom?"

The earl pretended to think. She was so beautiful, his Psyche, in her claret-colored wrapper with the white lace at the throat, her dark hair tumbling about her shoulders in riotous disorder. He

46

wanted to rush across the room, to hold her, to love her, to—*Slow down,* he told himself. *You must slow down.*

"No," he said finally. "I don't believe that was part of the treatment."

"Good. Because I am getting up."

"The Lindens said you would."

Psyche sent him a hard look. "The Lindens appear to have had a busy afternoon."

"Quite," agreed the earl. "One can hardly suffer boredom in their company."

Psyche snorted. "But one can suffer!"

He chuckled. "Then perhaps you're lucky to be up here instead of downstairs." He pulled a chair up to the bed and straddled it.

Psyche had a quick memory of the taut seat of his breeches just before she put her boot there. Gracious! What a thing to be thinking of!

He gave her a warm grin. "I told them they were wrong about everything regarding you, but especially about the bracket-faced thing."

She knew he was laughing at her and she wanted to laugh, too. Instead she pretended anger. "I do not need you to ride to my rescue."

Apparently he was not deceived. He chuckled again. "Not at the moment, perhaps. But you must admit that I did a good job this morning."

She couldn't help it: that charming smile of his called forth her own. "Yes, you make an excellent rescuer."

He smiled complacently. "I always knew you had good taste—and sense."

47

She looked at him curiously. "What do you mean—always? We only met yesterday."

He shrugged. "In person, yes. But when I was in Spain, I followed your escapades. With great delight, I might add. My mother used to write me about you."

Psyche did not want to pursue the subject. If only everyone would forget Lady Bluestocking. "I had hoped to come down to dinner. Lying abed is dreadfully dull business."

"Indeed it is," the earl agreed. "And I think you *should* come down." He gave her a sly look. "If you do not mind being pestered by the Lindens." He examined his cuffs. "I wish *I* had an excuse to avoid them. Too bad we can't stay up here and have a nice little tête-à-tête. It would be most amusing."

"Southdon." Overton stood in the doorway, wearing an annoyed frown. "Kindly give off practicing your wiles on Psyche. You know Lady Bluestocking is beyond that sort of thing."

Psyche swallowed a sharp retort. Why must everyone continually refer to Lady Bluestocking? Why couldn't they see that she wanted to put Lady Bluestocking behind her?

Slowly and surely the earl winked at her. But when he spoke, his voice was quite sober. "As you wish, Overton. As you wish." He leaned forward, lightly touching her cheek. "You will come down to dinner, won't you, my dear? Otherwise I shall be dreadfully disappointed." Then he was going, smiling gaily at them both, but leaving behind the warmth of his finger on her skin.

Overton frowned. "Southdon's a good enough chap," he said, advancing into the room. "But he has quite a name with the ladies. You should—"

"Overton!" What a worrier he had turned out to be. "There's no need to read me a lecture. I'm quite aware the earl's a charmer."

Overton nodded, but he still looked anxious. And if he pulled at his cravat much more it would come undone.

"You mustn't hold it against him," he said. "You know we men get used to behaving that way with females. We can't help it."

With some effort Psyche swallowed her irritation. Overton was actually putting himself into the same class as the earl! If she hadn't been so frustrated by her long lonely afternoon abed she might have been more amused. "I understand, cousin." She sighed. "I do want to come down to dinner. But those Lindens . . ."

Overton shrugged, avoiding her gaze. "They're busy relating all the latest *on-dits*. You know the sort."

"Only too well." Psyche straightened. There was something about his look, something evasive. "By the way, how do they know you asked me to manage Amanda's come-out?"

"I—I guess I told them. They wormed it out of me." Still avoiding her gaze, he edged closer to the door. "I'll see you at dinner." Then he, too, was gone.

Psyche reached for the bell cord. Since she was

going to dinner, she was going well dressed.

When the bell announced the dinner hour, Psyche was ready, dressed to the teeth in a gown of deep blue silk that Curtis swore was the loveliest she'd ever seen. Psyche supposed Overton would send some footmen to help her down to dinner. Since she had tried standing and found she was unable to take any steps alone, it seemed rather obvious she would not get downstairs if he didn't.

A soft rap sounded on the door. "Come in," she called.

The earl entered, smiling cheerfully. "Well, you are looking very fetching for an invalid."

Psyche tried not to return his smile, but she found it impossible. The man must be the greatest charmer alive. "I am not an invalid," she reminded him. "I am just a trifle indisposed. When Overton remembers to send some footmen, I shall be down for dinner."

The earl's eyes twinkled. "In that case I'm afraid you're going to be disappointed."

"What!" Overton couldn't be meaning to leave her there in her room! "You mean I can't go down to dinner?"

The earl gave her an amused glance. "My, my, like all your sex you seem prone to jump to conclusions."

"I'll tell you where I'll jump," Psyche threatened dramatically. "If I have to spend the entire evening shut up here, I'll jump out the window!"

The earl grinned. "Now, now, there's no need for such theatrics." He advanced toward the bed.

Psyche eyed him suspiciously. "I don't understand."

"I am here to carry you down to dinner." His grin broadened. "Never fear. Though you are no feather, I believe I can manage it."

"You don't say." She forced herself to ignore the wild antics of her heart. "I should prefer . . ." But she never got to finish the lie. The earl scooped her up into his arms. Psyche, her head against his waistcoat, could only sigh. She was, she reminded herself, a mature woman, used to handling her own affairs. Then why did being in the earl's arms make her feel so very young and giddy?

"You see," the earl said cheerfully, "I am as strong as any footman." He would never give this delightful task over to a footman. His arms had seemed empty since he'd let her out of them. And, though in truth, she was not exactly light, he would gladly have carried her anywhere. And soon—

The guests were gathered in the library, those Psyche had already seen and some newcomers. Overton's small house party was growing — growing too fast for her comfort.

The earl paused in the doorway to the library. When he looked down at her, the delightful man winked again. It was obvious he was enjoying setting them all on their ears. But when he spoke, his tone was sober. "I'm sure you'll all be delighted. Lady Psyche will be joining us for dinner after all."

Psyche, looking out into the curious faces, wondered what they were thinking. This was twice in one day that she had appeared before them cradled in the earl's arms. Across the room Miss Linden and her mother exchanged speaking glances. Psyche strongly suspected that only the hope of more scandal had kept them from rushing off to spread what they already knew.

She looked up at the man who carried her. "Why don't you put me down?"

"I prefer to hold you," he whispered with that fetching smile. It was so warm, so tender, that her bones felt like they'd melted and her heart began another series of wild palpitations.

Then she caught sight of Amanda's stricken face. "You must put me down," she told him firmly. "I shall explain later."

He shot her a quizzical glance. "Promise?"

"Of course."

He put her down then, but since he set her on her feet instead of depositing her in a chair, she was forced to lean rather heavily on his arm. It was a strong arm, well muscled. She could feel its hardness under her trembling fingers. And certainly leaning on it was a most pleasant experience, but she should not be thinking things like that.

Miss Linden approached, followed by her dragonish mama whose gown tonight looked like it had once been an awning and still contained sufficient yardage to revert to its original use. "My dear Lady Psyche," Lady Linden gushed. "I have not seen you for some time."

"I have been busy in the country," Psyche said, "managing my estate."

Lady Linden's eyes narrowed and her voice turned syrupy. "It's such a shame you have no husband to help you."

Psyche debated giving the old gossip a few sharp words, but, mindful of the avid listeners, she settled for saying, "I am quite capable of managing my own affairs, thank you."

Lady Linden actually smirked, quite an unattractive expression that did little to improve her looks. Then she nodded. "Except, of course, for marriage. My dear, I don't blame you for not wanting to help sweet Miss Caldecott find a husband. After all, you could not find one for yourself."

"Couldn't I?" Psyche could feel all their eyes upon her and she reacted automatically. She looked the huge harridan directly in the eye and said distinctly, "Miss Caldecott finds the estate of matrimony attractive. Lady Bluestocking despises it."

The earl, seeing all their shocked faces, cursed inwardly. The idiots would frighten her back into her Lady Bluestocking pose, into making those acerbic attacks on men and marriage. And that would mean more work for him, more wounds to heal before he could make her his wife.

He sighed. He *would* marry her. Someday. Somehow. He had promised himself that if he survived his wounds, if he reached England intact, he would have the woman he had loved for so long—and so secretly. But it would take patience—and he had never been a patient man.

Psyche kept her expression bland, but the shocked silence that followed her announcement was almost more embarrassing than Lady Linden's insults. Then the earl laughed and squeezed her hand. "Such a wit you are, Psyche."

His use of her Christian name raised eyebrows around the room, but that was not the worst of it. Psyche swallowed a bitter sigh. There would be no burying Lady Bluestocking now. She was back for good.

Chapter Five

The butler chose that moment, most opportunely to Psyche's way of thinking, to announce that dinner was served. He had scarcely finished when she felt the combined gazes of the guests return to her and her companion. The way they were staring at her, she might as well be the main attraction in a raree-show!

"If you'll just let me lean on you," she told the earl softly, "I believe I can walk to the table."

He frowned fiercely, his black eyebrows almost meeting over his nose. But though his frown was quite ferocious, his dark eyes were twinkling merrily. "Nonsense," he remarked, loud enough for all ears to hear. "I can carry you quite easily. And I—"

"Southdon, really—" Overton bustled up, frowning like a little old woman, and pulling at his cravat. He glanced around at the avidly watching guests and lowered his voice. "You are doing irreparable damage to Psyche's reputation, old man. If she must be carried, let a footman do it."

Psyche drew herself up. What a prig Overton was! And he far exceeded his authority, which did not in the least extend over her. "I thank you," she said haughtily, "for your cousinly concern, but I assure you that I am quite capable of looking out for my own reputation."

"Indeed," commented the earl dryly, "she is. Besides, how do you suppose Lady Bluestocking's reputation can be damaged? Her poor opinion of matrimony—and of men in general—is certainly well known."

And while her cousin gaped, openmouthed, the earl once more lifted Psyche into his arms.

She did not protest. Truly, she found walking very painful. And, just as truly, she found being in the earl's arms very pleasant. After all, if she decided to take on Amanda's come-out, she would have to spend a great deal of time in the earl's company, though not, regrettably, in his arms.

She was a practical person, she might as well enjoy his company while she could. But, she admitted to herself, enjoy was not precisely the word for the feelings she experienced, nestled there against the earl's brocade waistcoat.

It was strange that this man, this one particular man, should have such a peculiar effect on her. During her several seasons in town she had been besieged by men of all kinds. She had been pampered, courted, flattered, cajoled, humored, indulged, and doted on. But each man had seemed cut from the same cloth, and that cloth of a rather inferior quality.

The earl was different, though. He was a diamond of the first water, a top of the trees Corinthian, in manners and looks. But it wasn't only that. It was how he made her feel—strangely giddy, girlish, weak and helpless, yet strong and beautiful at the same time. Such foolishness, she chided herself. But she could not keep herself from delighting in the feel of the steady thud of his heart, his strong determined heart, beating under her hand. And even worse she could not prevent her own heart from palpitating wildly.

The earl, with her warm willowy body in his arms, tried not to smile in satisfaction. By the time her ankle had recovered, he intended to be much better acquainted with the beautiful Lady Bluestocking.

He carried her directly to the huge dinner table and deposited her at her place. Then while she watched, those lovely pansy eyes full of amusement, he calmly switched place cards with someone else, announcing, "Since I have appointed myself your transportation I must stay close at hand."

"Of course," Psyche answered, returning his smile. She had not smiled so much in many years. But that smile soon faded. Down the table Amanda was whispering to Overton, her pretty face contorted into a frown, her slim white fingers plucking nervously at a golden curl.

Psyche sighed. The girl was lovely. Bucks, young and old, would come flocking to pay court to her. Beautiful Amanda would have her pick of London's richest and finest. But she wanted London's best, she wanted the Earl of Southdon.

Psyche addressed herself to her tortoise soup. Why couldn't Amanda have wanted any other man in London? Why must the silly chit want this particular man?

The girl needed a good talking to. Perhaps then she'd set her sights on a target more appropriate to her tender years.

"Oh Mama, fie!" Miss Linden's staccato shriek pierced the convivial atmosphere of the dinner table and drew all attention in her direction. "I think that was all a mad, mad story. Even Lady Bluestocking wouldn't!" Here mother and daughter both sent Psyche a look that boded no good.

The earl swallowed a sigh. Psyche would not back down from anyone, least of all the odious Lindens, who were famous—or infamous—in all of London for their vast repertoire of scandalous *on-dits,* and the speed with which they disseminated them. It seemed everyone was determined to make his task harder.

He turned to watch. What would Psyche say now?

Miss Linden smiled and he was reminded of a cat about to pounce on an innocent mouse. "Lady Bluestocking would never say such a thing," she cooed. "Now would you?"

Psyche swallowed a pointed observation on Miss Linden's intellect—or lack thereof—and on the interesting possibilities of her parentage. Forcing herself to smile, she replied, "I'm afraid I can't say, since I don't know what it is that I—that Lady Bluestocking—is supposed to have said."

Miss Linden looked around the room in triumph, obviously pleased to have everyone's attention. Her thin lips curved into a smug smile. "Why, the story is that Lady Bluestocking, that *you,* told Lord Fetherill that a woman needs a husband like a fish needs—wings."

A shocked murmur sped around the table and then all was quiet as Overton's guests waited, their faces turned expectantly toward her.

"Surely you would not have said such an outrageous thing," Miss Linden continued. "I was just telling Mama so."

Well, Psyche thought, it was exactly as she'd feared. The Lindens meant to make all the trouble they could. But denying the truth would not prevent trouble, only increase it.

She kept her expression amused. "I'm dreadfully sorry to disappoint you, Miss Linden, but it appears that your mama is right. I distinctly remember making such a comment to Lord Fetherill." She managed a chuckle though she would far rather have strangled the stringy little gossip—and her fat toad of a mama, too. "If I remember rightly, he turned quite red, poor dear."

"But Lady Bluestock— Lady Psyche—" Lady Linden waved a pudgy hand, liberally ornamented with rings. "Surely you must recognize that women are weak creatures, the frail sex we are called."

A strange noise seemed to issue from the earl's vicinity, but when Psyche glanced his way he appeared quite composed and entirely engrossed in his partridge.

"Some women may be frail," she said stubbornly, looking directly at Lady Linden. "And obviously men are physically stronger than women, but I believe that some women are every bit as intelligent as some men."

"Hear, hear," whispered the earl, but only loud enough for Psyche's ears.

"I manage my estate quite well," she continued, warming to her topic, though she wasn't sure why. "Why should I desire to give it over to the control of some male who may well know less about managing it than I do?"

"Why indeed?" inquired the earl, sotto voce.

Lady Linden's expression vacillated between shock and satisfaction. Obviously she had hoped to goad Psyche into saying something of an inflammatory nature that could be spread around London. And just as obviously she had succeeded.

Miss Linden's colorless mouth snapped shut and her pale blue eyes blinked in surprise. "Oh my word, such shocking sentiments."

Psyche swallowed a sharp reply and kept her tongue firmly between her teeth.

Giggling girlishly, Aunt Anna patted the mauve ruffles that embellished her expansive bosom. "Oh my dear Miss Linden, Psyche always says shocking things. But she's a sweet girl anyhow. And she knows so much."

Aunt Anna frowned in puzzlement. "I never could figure out how sister's daughter could have such good understanding." She touched her frizzled blond hair, arranged in a style Psyche thought hideously uncomplimentary to her sallow face. "Sister and I, we were known for our beauty, not our brains. Not that Psyche isn't beautiful." She tittered. "She's quite an attractive girl in her own way."

She stopped, waving a hand in an aimless circle, then pressing it to her brow. "Oh dear! And now I've lost track of what I meant to tell you."

"Perhaps," said Lady Linden, her round face creasing into a satisfied smile, "perhaps it had to do with Lady Psyche's fortune-telling. Earlier today you mentioned that she can tell amazing things about the future. And with just a deck

61

of playing cards."

"Oh yes!" Aunt Anna cried, clapping her hands. "She can!"

Psyche swallowed an urge to garnish Lady Linden's more than ample bosom with the remains of her tortoise soup. She'd been quite right in her supposition. As usual, the Lindens were out to make trouble. Unfortunately, she had no means to stop them.

"My dear," Aunt Anna cried, her eyes sparkling, "after dinner you simply must amuse us."

"I'm afraid I have no playing cards," Psyche said, careful to keep the satisfaction out of her voice. She sent a speaking look to Overton, silently imploring him *not* to produce a deck of cards.

Beside her, the earl frowned. It was obvious to him that Psyche didn't want to tell fortunes. It was equally obvious that the Lindens would continue to harass her until they trapped her into more Lady Bluestocking *bon mots*. Surely telling fortunes from cards would be the safer pastime.

He smiled to himself. If Psyche told fortunes, he could assist her. He could carry her about. And he could get her to read the cards for him. She would not be able to escape him — at least not for the space of her fortune-telling. And the Lindens would not get any more ammunition to use against her. Psyche was not to be trifled with. Not when he was present, at least.

When the Lindens said nothing, Psyche heaved a sigh of relief. Apparently they had no cards either. They were foiled—at least for the moment.

And then from beside her, from the last person she would have expected to give any help to the Lindens, came a deep chuckle. "I have a deck of playing cards," the earl said, "quite new, in fact. And I shall be pleased to offer them to Lady Psyche if she will entertain us later."

His smile was all graciousness, but his eyes were twinkling again. What strange ideas of amusement the man had.

But she knew she was fairly caught. Glancing down the table she saw Aunt Anna beaming happily, Gresham nodding enthusiastically, and Georgie clapping her hands in glee. "It will be capital fun," Georgie cried. "Psyche is really very good at it."

Psyche, stealing a glance at the Lindens, found them both wearing complacent smiles. And no wonder. They had achieved their end and now would be able to bruit it about London that Lady Bluestocking was up to her old tricks.

Smiling, Aunt Anna returned to her dinner, Georgie turned to converse again with Gresham, and Amanda resumed her agitated discussion with her guardian, the subject of which Psyche feared was the distressing conduct of her new mentor. Psyche resumed eating her partridge.

"Your popularity spreads," the earl remarked softly, leaning toward her.

She fixed him with a gimlet eye, trying to appear incensed. But he was such a devilishly attractive man with his eyes sparkling in that mischievous way and his lips curling into that appealing smile that she found her own lips trying to curve into an answering smile.

Still, she tried to be stern. "Perhaps," she told him, "I do not wish to tell fortunes. Didn't that occur to you?"

"No." He appeared genuinely surprised. "It didn't. Why ever not? As Georgie says, it sounds like great fun."

She wrinkled her nose. "For you, perhaps. But tell me"—she lowered her voice—"why do you abet the Lindens in their infamous behavior?"

He shrugged his shoulders, reminding her again of their considerable breadth. "Perhaps I wished to see you in action." He grinned. "Or perhaps I wanted to discover *my* future."

"I can tell you your future without cards," she said darkly. "You will come to no good end."

He chuckled. "Because I have aided and abetted the enemy?"

She knew she was smiling, yet she was unable to stop. "Precisely. If you had kept quiet, I could have avoided this tangle."

He shrugged. "Perhaps. But to what end?"

She stared at him. "To what end? To the end

of not adding to Lady Bluestocking's already more than adequate notoriety."

His eyes danced. "Do you seriously believe you can keep the Lindens from spreading gossip about you?"

She smiled grimly. "Not unless they are both taken deathly ill and rendered mute."

He raised an eyebrow. "Then why not amuse the rest of us with your talents?"

Why not, indeed. She supposed her reluctance must seem peculiar to him. "You see— It's just— I had hoped to leave Lady Bluestocking buried, keep her out of my return to London. Resurrection of the Bluestocking stories will hardly increase Amanda's matrimonial chances, you know."

He looked at her over the rim of his wine-glass. "Does that mean you have made up your mind, you have decided to take on the come-out?"

She nodded, the decision made. "Yes, it's quite foolish of me I suppose, but I have always risen to a challenge. In effect the Lindens have dared me to do it. And so I feel I must."

He seemed to consider this for some moments while he ate. Then he turned to her and raised a dark eyebrow. "So, did someone dare you to become Lady Bluestocking?"

She sighed, wishing for the hundredth time that the Lindens had let Lady Bluestocking lie— dead and buried—and quite forgotten. "No," she said. "It just—sort of happened."

That was not precisely the truth. It had just—sort of—happened because she had *made* it happen. She had set out deliberately to make herself the talk of the town, and she had succeeded beyond her fondest aspirations. Lady Bluestocking's escapades, her antimarriage sentiments, her diatribes against husbands, her acid recriminations against the male half of the species, were recounted far and near, whispered about in every fashionable club and drawing room in London—and far beyond.

She had achieved the effect she desired, convincing her suitors that she was not suitable wifely material, that marriage to her, in spite of her rather large fortune, would be more trouble than it was worth.

She sipped her wine. What a pity the earl hadn't been around then. Lady Bluestocking might never have seen the light of day if the handsome, witty earl had been there to trade badinage and warm looks with her.

But of course the present warmth in his looks was entirely due to his friendship with Overton. She was, after all, cousin to Overton, and so the earl would exert himself to keep her amused. And, of course, being Lady Bluestocking, she was safe company. There was nothing more to it than that. She was going to London to arrange Amanda's come-out, after all, not to embark on some husband-hunting jaunt of her own. Lady Bluestocking would never find a husband. She had seen to that five years ago.

A lump rose in her throat, making it temporarily difficult to swallow. How silly people could be, believing every ridiculous thing she said—or at least believing *she* believed it.

Chapter Six

After dinner, the gentlemen, eager to hear their fortunes read, decided by common consent to forego their port. The earl dispatched a footman to his room to acquire the playing cards from his valet. Then he lifted Psyche again and carried her back to the library.

He paused in the doorway, looking down at her with sparkling eyes. "Where do you wish to be deposited?" he inquired.

Psyche found it difficult to behave normally, as though they were just making polite conversation, when all the time this most attractive man had one arm under her knees and the other around her back, when her cheek was resting against his shoulder, and his darkly handsome face was so close to hers that her heart wanted to jump out of her bosom.

She tried to think sensibly, but it was not easy. "I don't know. I shall need a table—to lay out the cards. And something to sit on."

He nodded. "Perhaps the sofa is best for you.

You will be more comfortable there with your foot up."

"Yes, I suppose so." She appreciated the earl's concern for her. Goodness, without him she'd be stuck up there in her room, with only Curtis for company. Still, it did seem that he was carrying his friendship for Overton a little far, especially considering her cousin's prudish anxiety over reputations.

Then she had another thought. Perhaps this was not a thing of friendship, perhaps the earl was ragging his friend. These London bucks did like to tease each other. And Overton certainly had a tendency to get flustered, to be overmuch concerned with propriety.

As though her thoughts had summoned him, Overton crossed the room, his forehead wrinkled in a worried frown. "Really, Psyche," he said, pulling at his cravat. "Don't you think this is a trifle excessive?"

From her place in the earl's arms, Psyche gave him a hard look. "Indeed, I do. But it was *your* guests and *your* mama who insisted upon my doing it."

Overton looked pained. "I did not mean— That is, I meant—"

Oh no, Psyche thought, averting her gaze, not another scold. The Lindens already had sufficient verbal ammunition to keep the ton talking about her for months on end. What could being carried one more time add to that?

The earl frowned. Overton was overdoing this

69

propriety thing. If he didn't want the Lindens spreading their malicious tales throughout the ton, he should have countermanded his mother's invitation and sent the pair packing. Two unlikelier, more unwelcome, house guests had seldom been seen. And Overton had played right into their hands.

The earl fixed the man with a grave look. "Psyche's right. What else could she do when everyone asked her? You *were* talking about the fortune-telling, weren't you?"

With a look at Psyche, Overton sighed sheepishly.

The man had not been thinking of fortune-telling, the earl thought. That was plain enough. Overton had been thinking of the impropriety of one of his male guests carrying one of his female guests about. Well, he could fret all he wanted. If Psyche needed carrying, it would be done by the man who loved her.

Overton pulled at his cravat again. "Yes, of course. Really, Psyche, I am only thinking of Amanda, you know. The ton can be very hard on—"

"Indeed, I know," Psyche interjected smoothly. "And because of that perhaps you had best let your mama handle Amanda's—"

"No!" Overton glanced around, frowning.

She was good, the earl thought. She knew how to bring Overton around.

The earl smiled. He hadn't done so badly himself. Overton was convinced that Psyche was the one to handle Amanda's come-out. And that had been no small feat, though knowing Overton's esteemed mama's alarming proclivities had helped considerably.

Overton sighed again and went on in a lower voice. "I want you to do the come-out. The girl needs a good husband and you're the one to find him for her. I want Amanda to have the best."

Psyche swallowed a sigh. Overton and his ward were agreed on that one thing, at least. Unfortunately agreed. She could understand a schoolroom girl, which was what Amanda really still was, falling head over heels for the handsome, dashing earl. But Overton ought to know better than to encourage her. What had possessed her cousin to think that Amanda, that green girl, would suit the earl? Why, he'd be bored with her in one night, at the most two. And then what would the child do?

The earl put Psyche on the sofa. "You'll be comfortable here," he said, bending to pile pillows behind her back and more under her injured ankle to properly elevate it.

She saw Georgie sending her knowing looks. And Amanda was frowning fiercely. Psyche avoided her gaze, trying to think about something else. But unfortunately, what she thought about was not any less disturbing. She was actually sorry to be out of the earl's arms. She had been quite comfortable there. Well, not exactly comfortable, but happy. Now she was experiencing a most peculiar sense of loss and an intense desire

71

to be that near him again. This was insanity! She must forget such thoughts immediately.

The earl smiled down at her. "I shall find the table and chairs you require."

As he moved away, the others pulled their chairs into a circle, curiosity on their faces. Except for Amanda. She looked like she'd eaten too many green apples. They must have a talk—and soon. No man would wish to marry a woman who went around looking like she had a perpetual stomachache.

The earl returned, carrying a small fluted table whose pedestaled base looked like the foot of some great leviathan. Psyche smiled. Aunt Anna's taste in furniture had always leaned toward the Egyptian, but this table was grotesque. The earl put it beside the sofa, then placed a lyre-back chair on the other side of it.

He set another chair at the foot of the sofa, facing Psyche, and with a satisfied smile sat down, saying, "For tonight consider me your servant. I shall be completely at your beck and call."

Psyche tried not to smile foolishly at the man. Probably she should discourage him. But how to do it? He did not seem a man who discouraged easily and he had certainly been persistent in his attentions. Had this been her Season or had he not known her identity as Lady Bluestocking, she might easily have deceived herself into believing that he had a tendre for her.

But this was *not* her Season and he *did* know her identity, so that could not be the reason for his attentions to her. And then she realized what the reason was! It came to her with all the suddenness — and the pain — of a stubbed toe.

The earl was cultivating her acquaintance because he knew she was going to manage Amanda's come-out. Knowing Amanda's chaperone would give him the inside track in the matrimonial sweepstakes. As if he needed it!

Yes, that must be it. Knowing Overton's skittishness about reputations, the earl had thought it wise to take precautions, to ingratiate himself with Psyche so that she would be on his side. That was certainly prudent of him — and reasonable. Then why did it make her want to cry? To stamp her foot and run off to her room in a fit of petulance?

Of course she could do neither and so she sat, struggling to get herself in hand. Now that she had discovered his real intentions, she surveyed the earl with a jaundiced eye, seeking his faults. But there was certainly nothing to fault in his looks. The best legs in London were now gracefully crossed, admirably broad shoulders leaned back against his chair. He had a very handsome if somewhat commanding face, and a low vibrant voice that could echo deep in a woman's bones. As for his behavior —

The footman appeared with the deck of cards and silently handed them to the earl.

"Who shall be first?" he inquired politely, turning to face the others.

"Me! Oh me!" squealed the stickish Miss Linden, smoothing the skirt of her Grecian gown. The girl was too young and too thin for the Greek style. Its severe lines did little to make her more attractive. She looked like a little girl masquerading as a grown-up lady.

Handing Psyche the cards, the earl slowly winked. This evening was going to be fun. He meant to stay close to her, for as long as he could.

He got up. "Sit right here, Miss Linden. Allow me to help you."

Miss Linden lowered her gaze and flushed clear to her pale forehead. "Oh, milord, you're most kind."

He pushed her up to the table and then turned back to the sofa. He leaned over, examining Psyche's foot where it lay propped up among the pillows. He tugged a pillow a few inches to one side. Actually, it was not the pillows he wanted to touch, but Psyche herself. She looked so fetching, lying there like that. Almost as he had pictured her in Spain, only then he had not imagined her on a sofa.

Psyche shuffled the cards and, seeing the red stain spreading on Amanda's pale cheeks, wished herself someplace else, any place else. "I am fine," she snapped at the earl. "Quite comfortable. Kindly sit down."

The earl raised a surprised eyebrow at this unprovoked waspishness, but remained silent, resuming his seat.

Psyche sighed. What was she to do? She was

not a quitter. She had never been a quitter. And she certainly had no intention of letting the despicable Lindens drive her back to the country.

Imagine those two thinking themselves responsible for her departure from town! She'd been bored, that's all, tired of town life—the patent artificiality, the glittering false world of *on-dits* and scandal where kindness was a flaw and lies and innuendo everyday fare. So she had gone back to her estate in Sussex, lived there quite comfortably, too, until Overton had come to disrupt her orderly, if somewhat lonely, existence with his pleas for help.

She dealt out thirteen cards, face up in a circle, then put three more, face down, inside it.

Miss Linden leaned forward, her expression eager, her pale hands plucking nervously at each other. How strange that such a girl should put store in this kind of thing.

Psyche looked down at the circle of cards. "Ten of clubs," she said. "Beware, a popular young woman you know is not to be trusted."

Miss Linden's pale brow furrowed. She was reviewing her so-called friends, Psyche thought, and probably mistrusting every one of them. "Eight of spades," Psyche continued. "Unless you are careful you will lose a friend through selfishness." Surely that was likely, *if* the girl had any friends to begin with. She moved on to the next card. "Five of diamonds. You will inherit something of value."

Miss Linden's plain face brightened. "Can you

75

tell me what it is?"

Psyche shook her head. "The cards don't say." She continued her reading, ending with the last of the thirteen cards. "Five of clubs. Someone will try to get you to repeat gossip. Pretend you know nothing and save yourself a lot of trouble." Excellent advice, Psyche told herself, but clearly wasted on someone of Miss Linden's ilk.

Miss Linden gnawed on her lower lip. "Is there— Is there nothing of a romantic nature in the cards?"

Psyche frowned. "Not here." So, even Miss Linden wished for a husband. Too bad, with a mother like hers she certainly had little chance of getting married. Poor thing. Pity stirred in Psyche's heart. She knew what it was like to have the wrong kind of mama. Being Lady Linden's daughter must be far from pleasant.

"Things of a romantic nature," Psyche explained, "usually occur in the suit of hearts." She reached for the cards in the middle. "Perhaps one of these will indicate—" She turned it over.

"A heart," Miss Linden crowed. "The four!"

"Which indicates the marriage of a close relative."

Miss Linden's face fell. It was clear she wished for a marriage somewhat closer, like her own.

Psyche turned over another card.

"The king!" Miss Linden cried, clapping her hands. "Is that good?"

Psyche nodded. "Very good. A blond man secretly admires you."

Miss Linden's sallow face took on a rosy cast. "A blond man," she breathed. "One more card. I do hope it's a good one."

Psyche turned it over. "The five of hearts. You will take a long trip."

Miss Linden looked disappointed. Poor girl, Psyche thought, surprised by another surge of pity. "You will take this trip alone," she continued, somewhat to her amazement extemporizing for the girl's benefit. "Except, of course, for your maid. And on this trip you will meet a wonderful, wonderful man."

There! Psyche told herself. That should give Miss Linden something worthwhile to think about. And Lady Linden, too!

Looking stunned, Miss Linden remained in her chair. "A trip," she mumbled. "A wonderful man."

Aunt Anna bustled up, like some gigantic mauve tent bedecked with ruffles. "Come, my dear," she said gently, pulling Miss Linden to her feet and leading her aside. "Psyche has many futures to read yet. Now who wants to be next?"

"I do," cried Georgie, from her place across the circle. Smiling at Gresham and the others, she bounced over to sit at the little table.

As Psyche shuffled the cards and dealt them out, Georgie grinned. "So, Psyche, do you read good things in my future?"

Psyche smiled. In spite of Georgie's flirtatious attentions to the earl, they were still friends. Georgie couldn't help her nature. "Indeed, I do."

77

It was easy to predict Georgie's good fortune, even without the cards. Georgie was the kind who always landed on her feet.

The first card up was the ace of hearts. "Life-long happiness with the one you love," Psyche said. "What more could you ask for?"

"Nothing," Georgie returned with a seductive smile at the earl. "Nothing at all."

Psyche stifled a sigh. That was Georgie, always flirting. But must she do it with the earl? Did she have to want him, too?

She must stop this kind of thinking, Psyche told herself harshly. If the earl decided to marry, he—and he alone—would decide who the lady was to be. And no one and nothing could change that.

When the reading of her cards was finished, Georgie tripped back to her seat. Beaming, she stopped to speak to Gresham, laying a familiar hand on his shoulder. "You're next."

Gresham sauntered across the room, flirting shamelessly with Psyche, and ogling her up and down. The earl straightened in his chair. If he hadn't known the man was besotted with Georgie, he might have really bristled. As it was, he still felt a sense of disquiet. Lady Bluestocking was *his,* even if she didn't know it yet. He didn't want other men flattering her, even in fun.

Leaning forward, Gresham eyed Psyche. "Do you see yourself in my future, oh beautiful one?"

Psyche chuckled and raised an eyebrow. "I'm afraid not, milord. But your future looks bright."

She touched the ace of clubs. "This denotes great success socially." She smiled. "Of course that's no surprise—a man with your silver tongue should have no problems."

Gresham preened a little, and ran a hand through his reddish hair.

The earl forced himself to relax. Gresham *was* mad about Georgie. He was no threat.

"Do go on," Gresham said.

"The ace of diamonds. You will achieve wealth by hard and honest work."

Both Gresham's eyebrows shot up. "Work! Me? Impossible!" He put a hand over his extravagantly brocaded waistcoat, clutching dramatically at his heart. "I assure you I have never worked a day in my life!"

Psyche laughed with the rest of them, the earl saw. But that light wasn't shining in her eyes, the light that shone there when she looked at *him*. "Then perhaps," she said, "your wealth will come from someone else's hard and honest work."

Gresham chuckled, his round face jovial, his eyes merry. "That's more like it. I am always willing to profit from someone else's labor."

Chapter Seven

One by one, Psyche read their fortunes — all but Lady Linden's and the earl's. Lady Linden pleaded a headache and went early up to bed, dragging her still dazed daughter after her. The others gradually drifted away, leaving the earl and Psyche alone in that part of the room.

She gazed at him speculatively. "How is this? I thought you wished to have your fortune told, but you did not take your turn with the others."

He hitched his chair closer and took her hand. That was highly improper, of course. She sought to withdraw her fingers from his grasp, but he didn't allow it. "Wait," he said, holding them more tightly still. "I wish to tell *your* fortune."

"The cards are on the table," she replied, a little stiffly because actually she did not want to withdraw her hand at all. It felt quite natural in his, as though it belonged there. "You must shuffle them first, though."

He shook his head, his dark eyes gleaming. "No, Psyche, not with the cards. I mean to read your palm."

A shiver sped down her spine, whether from the way he spoke her name or from the way he was holding her hand she couldn't be sure. "I didn't know— How did you learn to read palms?"

He smiled at her. "When I was a boy, the Gypsies camped on our summer estate. I used to watch them read my mother's hand. And those of the servants. It was great fun."

She tried to protest, tried to pull her hand away. "But that doesn't mean—"

"I know enough," he said softly, turning her palm over. He traced a line down it with his warm forefinger. Another shiver afflicted her. This was ridiculous. She was no schoolroom chit to be thrown into the vapors by the touch of a man's finger!

"This, this is your lifeline," he went on in that deep voice of his. "It shows your life will be long." He leaned closer still and a certain giddiness overtook her, a longing to topple into his arms.

Be sensible, she told herself. *He's merely playing with you, doing what he does best.* But oh, if only he weren't playing, if only he were serious.

The earl tried to remain calm. He had reached her. She had that look in her eyes, that look that he knew preceded surrender. But this was no game of flirtation he was playing. This was the most serious thing in his life. She held his future in her hand, all right, but not in any lines. And it was still too soon. He dared not ask her yet.

He hitched his chair a little closer. "And this is your love line. It's very strong. I see marriage, one marriage, to a man you love." If only he could tell her, *he* was the man. How much longer could he bear to wait? But he must not make the attempt too early.

Psyche threw him a hard look, and pulled her hand away. "Enough foolishness," she cried. "I am too fatigued for this."

Across the room, Aunt Anna looked up. "You should be abed," she cried, bustling over. "I'm sorry, my dear, I have been remiss keeping you up so late after your injury."

Perversely, now that she had an excuse to leave the others, Psyche found that she didn't want to do it. "I—"

"Psyche has not yet read the cards for me," the earl told Aunt Anna, his eyes full of laughter. "Surely you would not deprive me of that pleasure?"

Aunt Anna giggled. The earl had that effect on women, Psyche thought with some bitterness. No matter their age—or size—he made them act like green girls just out of the schoolroom.

"Very well," Aunt Anna said. "But then Psyche really must go up to her room. We can't have her taking ill, you know."

The earl nodded. "Word of honor."

When Aunt Anna seemed disposed to linger, he turned his charming smile on her again. "I have waited till last," he said softly, "because I wish for a private reading. You do understand?"

Aunt Anna blushed rosy red. "Of course, of course." And she bustled off.

"Aunt Anna may understand," Psyche said crisply when her aunt was out of earshot. "But I do not. First you wish your fortune told, then you don't, then you do again."

He smiled at her, that smile that made her bones want to melt into nothing. "May a man not change his mind as easily as a woman?"

Psyche frowned. "I suppose *a man* may do anything he chooses."

A faint hint of color rose to the earl's cheeks and a muscle twitched in his jaw. "Ah, so you dislike the way men run the world."

"I do, indeed!" Psyche leaped into battle. "Men have made a royal mess of things. Why, look at that Frenchman Bonaparte, attacking us, thinking he can conquer England."

"And how would *you* have things run?" the earl inquired dryly.

Psyche shook back her curls. "By a woman," she declared. "A woman like good Queen Bess. After all, in her time we stopped the Spanish Armada."

The earl smiled. "You're right, of course. But come." He picked up the cards and pushed them into her hands. "Shuffle, please. I am eagerly awaiting word of my future."

Psyche took the cards reluctantly. She didn't know why her hands wanted to tremble. Reading the cards was a trick, an illusion, a ruse. She knew that. So did he.

She shuffled the cards again and began to lay them out. The earl chuckled. "The five of hearts. Shall *I* take a long trip, alone of course, and meet a wonderful woman?"

"I think not," Psyche said, refusing to smile. "You have already made a long trip to get here."

83

"I see." He beamed at her across the little table. Why must he be such a wonderful-looking man? A man who made her feel alive and happy. A man she would like to spend forever— Enough, she told herself sharply. It was foolish to dream of such impossibilities.

She turned up the six of spades. "Your temper will get you in trouble unless you are careful."

"*My* temper," he said, raising an eyebrow. "*My* temper is one of the evenest. Now your temper—"

She refused to be baited. She refused to smile, too. He was only playing with her, sharpening his drawing-room skills on her. And only because she was Lady Bluestocking, and her poor opinion of men—and marriage—was so well known. If he ever suspected her real feelings, that at this very moment she longed to be in his arms . . .

She turned up another card. "Six of hearts. Someone will do you a personal favor for which you must take care to express your appreciation."

He grinned brashly. "Are you quite certain this is *my* fortune you are telling?"

"Quite certain," she repeated, unable to meet his eyes. She was suddenly aware that she was being churlish. No doubt, as Overton had pointed out, the earl treated all women with this friendly raillery. Perhaps she had been too long in the country. It was foolish of her to take his actions so personally.

She forced herself to smile while she reported on the rest of the cards and the earl accepted their interpretations in silence.

Then Psyche reached for the first of the turned-down cards. "Perhaps," he said, "we should stop now, leave well enough alone."

"Oh no!" She forced her voice to gaiety. "You must have your *whole* fortune read." She turned over the first card. "The ace of hearts."

"The same fortune as Georgie's," the earl murmured, glancing to where she was flirting with Gresham.

"Yes." Somehow Psyche managed a smile, managed to get the words out. "Lifelong happiness with the one you love." Fortune-telling was a ridiculous business. Just because his fortune was the same as Georgie's — Just because Georgie looked at him that way — She turned over another card.

"Three of hearts. A situation will soon arise in which you will have to choose between sentiment and business."

When he didn't comment on that, she reached for the last card. "Queen of hearts. A blond woman secretly admires you."

She was watching his eyes, his dark, expressive eyes. They didn't move away from hers, didn't seek Amanda's blond, youthful beauty across the room. Or Georgie's more sophisticated allure. But the corner of his mouth twitched and he raised a quizzical eyebrow.

Silently Psyche gathered the cards and returned them to him. "I find I am very tired," she said. "Will you ask Overton to send a footman to help me up to bed?"

"No, I will not." His gaze didn't leave hers. "You see I rather like the job. And I do not intend to give it up."

She was too tired to continue this game. "You will give Overton apoplexy if you continue to carry me about. To say nothing of what the Lindens will make of it."

He shrugged. "I have already carried you — to the horse, to the library, up to your room, down to the library, in to dinner, back from dinner — How can one more carrying do any harm? Besides, the Lindens have already retired to their rooms."

Psyche sighed. There was a certain perverted sense to his logic. Besides, perhaps being once more in his arms she could dispel these foolish girlish notions and remember that she was a mature woman who had promised to help Amanda Caldecott get the husband she wanted. "Very well."

So, once more the earl gathered Psyche in his arms. He congratulated himself on his good fortune. He should thank his lucky stars for that mishap she'd had with the building stone. He would never have gotten this close to her otherwise, his prickly Lady Bluestocking.

She fit so perfectly in his arms, his delightful Psyche, his acerbic Psyche. As perfectly as she fit in his heart. And he would make her love him. He must. Because now that he had spent time with her, he was more convinced than ever. He loved her. He wanted to make her his wife.

He waited while she made her good nights, then moved toward the stairs, carrying his precious burden. The surgeon had assured him that her ankle was only twisted and that keeping off it would effect a cure. He didn't want her to be incapacitated, of course, but he would dearly love the chance to carry her longer.

Her head rested against his shoulder, her scent teased his nostrils. Had she been any other woman he would have succumbed to the temptation and kissed her, right there in the upstairs hall. But this was Lady Bluestocking—and he did not dare. Not yet.

He suspected, indeed, he was almost positive, that her intense dislike of men and marriage had been a facade, erected to protect herself from the sort of suitors that her mother had pressed on her. Poor darling, to be so hard put to keep from marrying.

And yet how fortunate for him. If one of them had succeeded, Psyche would be forever beyond his reach. Instead she was there, so temptingly there, in his arms.

Chapter Eight

Psyche woke to morning sunlight streaming into her room. She sighed and stretched. She had not spent a restful night. Indeed, with so much tossing and turning it was a wonder she hadn't injured herself even further.

She closed her eyes, remembering the night before, remembering the earl. After she'd made her good nights to the other guests, enduring Georgie's raised eyebrow, Gresham's knowing grin, and Amanda's pained frown, the earl had dutifully carried her back up the stairs to her room.

As she had promised herself she would, she tried very hard to rid herself of the strange feelings that being so near the man incited in her. When he lifted her from the sofa, gathering her again in his arms, she tried very, very hard. But no matter how she tried or how she warned herself that this kind of thinking was the most unutterable folly, she still wanted to be there, held in the earl's arms, cradled against his waistcoat. It was sheer stupidity, but she simply couldn't help it.

The earl paused outside her chamber door, waiting till Curtis opened it for him. And Psyche wished that Curtis would, just this once, be remiss in her duties so that the moment might last longer. But alas, Curtis, as conscientious as ever, came at the first call.

The earl carried Psyche to the bed, putting her gently down on the pink silken coverlet. He bent low, his handsome face only inches from hers. "Do you need anything else?" he asked softly. "If you do, I shall be glad to get it for you."

"No, no. You have — been most — kind." Her tongue wanted to stumble over the simplest words and her heart had leapt up into her throat and was bouncing around there like a mad thing. "Thank you."

For another long moment he remained bent over her, his face close to hers, his mouth mere inches away. She felt his breath on her cheek, inhaled the hint of spice and leather. And then, when she thought she couldn't bear another instant of this exquisite torture, he straightened. "Sleep well, Psyche. Good night."

"Good night." She watched him go, his back so straight, his figure so manly, his stride so determined. And she sighed. Like the greenest schoolroom chit, she sighed.

Curtis shut the door after him and scurried back to the bed, her eyes bright with curiosity. "Oh my, milady, he's a real looker, that earl is. But," she frowned, pulling off Psyche's slippers and setting them side by side on the floor, "but I heard tell he's quite a hand with the ladies. One of them ladies is always thinking she's going to marry him, but ain't none of 'em managed it. And from the looks of him, they won't." She straightened, hands on hips. "That's a man what'll choose his own woman. And have his pick of 'em, too."

Psyche finally found her tongue. "Curtis," she said crisply, "we won't discuss my cousin's guests."

" 'Course not," Curtis replied complacently, undoing Psyche's hooks and helping her out of her gown and into her nightdress. "Still, milady, I've got to say it. Was I a lady of any kind, and a man like that was to come near me—" She grinned. "Why, I'd do everything I could think of to get him to marry me."

Frowning, Psyche lay back against her pillows. Even the servants were mesmerized by the earl's insistent charm. Well, at least she would be prepared. She would not be surprised when he asked for Amanda's hand. Still, she could not help thinking that his marriage to Amanda would be a mistake, a great mistake. A man like the earl would expect conversation with his wife, conversation of some depth. How, for example, could Amanda discuss antiquities with him?

Psyche sighed and stretched again, opening her eyes. Last night's questions had had no answers then; they had no answers now. And all the time she'd spent lying awake trying to find answers had been a pure waste—of time and energy. If

90

she wasn't careful, she would indeed be bracket-faced! If only from lack of sleep.

She stretched again and bent her ankle. It felt surprisingly well, considering. Perhaps she'd be able to stand on it. She threw back the covers and put her bare feet to the floor. One step, then another. Her ankle felt a little stiff, but otherwise everything was fine.

She sighed again, almost disappointed. Disappointed! What foolishness! She could not be having the earl carry her around all the time. It was not dignified. And besides, it was too disconcerting, too disturbing, too — pleasant. And there was Amanda to consider.

Psyche sighed deeply. She couldn't put it off any longer. She must dress now and have a serious talk with the girl.

The breakfast room was deserted when Psyche arrived there, but the sideboard held enough food to feed an army. She filled a plate and sat down; eating alone was no novelty to her.

When she had finished, she sat back with a cup of tea and summoned a footman. "Find Miss Caldecott and tell her I wish to speak to her in my room, as soon as possible."

The footman nodded. "Yes, milady."

Psyche finished her tea and started back up the stairs. This coming interview with Amanda was not going to be pleasant. She could not even be sure the girl had enough understanding to follow what she was going to try to tell her. Certainly Amanda had not seemed particularly bright so far.

Mounting the great staircase, Psyche sighed. The earl was going to be so bored, so overcome with ennui— That is, if he decided to marry Amanda.

What a tangle! To make Amanda happy she must make the earl unhappy. Not on purpose, of course. But how could the man be happy leg-shackled to a veritable child? Some men, of course, preferred young brides, gullible girls who could easily be trained to obedience.

Psyche snorted and nearly missed a step. Obedience, indeed! The very idea put women on par with animals. It was indecent. And it did not seem like the kind of thing the earl would do.

She reached her room, sent Curtis on an errand, and settled down on the chaise longue to wait.

She didn't wait long. Five minutes later a knock sounded. "Come in," Psyche called, bracing herself.

The door opened and Amanda said stiffly, "Did you wish to see me?"

"Yes," Psyche said. "Come over here and sit down."

Amanda came slowly, her face showing reluctance.

"Pull up that chair," Psyche said. "We need to talk."

Amanda pulled up the chair and perched on

the edge of it, obviously ready to take flight.

"You are upset with me," Psyche said. "Because the earl has been carrying me about."

Amanda nodded, twisting her ribbons. "Yes, I am! I don't see how you can expect him to ask to marry me when he's always carting you about. It— It doesn't look good."

Psyche sighed. Overton's sentiments, no doubt. "It does look strange," she admitted. "But the earl is a friend of Overton and I am Overton's cousin."

"I know that," Amanda said. "But you still don't have to let the earl carry you about."

Psyche swallowed a sigh. "He won't be carrying me anymore. You'll be pleased to hear that my ankle is better today and I can walk by myself. You see, the earl was just being friendly, helpful."

Amanda's pink lips pursed in a pout. *"Very* friendly. Lady Linden says—"

"Lady Linden!" Psyche rubbed her temples, where a great headache hovered, ready to pounce. "How can you possibly believe that horrible woman?" She threw her arms heavenward, her patience exhausted. "Fine! Ask *her* to manage your come-out!"

Amanda's pout vanished and her face crumpled into tears. "Oh no, not Lady Linden! She's just terrible. I couldn't stand it." Tears stood in her bright blue eyes. "Oh, milady, please help me. I know I'm a foolish girl. But I do love him so."

Psyche swallowed another sigh, her head beginning to pound. What did this child know of love?

"Amanda, love isn't always the best measure of happiness. I know you want to marry the earl, but think— Would you be happy with him?" She paused, but Amanda didn't answer. "Wouldn't you have a more pleasant existence with a man nearer your own age?"

Amanda's blue eyes widened. She sniffled and twisted her handkerchief, avoiding Psyche's gaze. Then she said, "Milady, I don't want to marry the earl."

Psyche's heart threatened to jump right out of her mouth. She almost leaped to her feet to shout with joy. But could she possibly be hearing right? "You don't? But you said—"

"I said I want him to *ask* me," Amanda explained patiently, as though to an ignorant child. "But I don't really want to marry him."

Psyche stared at the girl in bewilderment. "Amanda, please, if I'm to help you I've got to understand this. You want the earl to propose marriage to you and then you intend to refuse him?"

Amanda nodded, her blond curls bobbing emphatically. "That's right, milady."

Psyche shook her head. "But why?"

Amanda's tears threatened to overflow. "So that *he* will be jealous, of course. So that *he* will ask me to marry *him*."

Psyche frowned. "Amanda, make some sense here. Who is this *he?*"

Amanda glanced around her. "You won't tell anyone? You promise?" She lowered her voice.

94

"He must never know that I love him. Not unless he loves me."

Psyche nodded. "All right, I promise. Now, who is this mystery man?"

"Overton," Amanda whispered. "I love my guardian, Overton."

Shock sent Psyche into momentary silence. Overton! Amanda loved Overton! My God, the chit had some sense after all. It was Overton who was lacking in brains. Why hadn't he seen that Amanda cared for him? But then, if he limited his visits to twice a year—

Psyche smiled, her headache retreating. "I think I begin to see your intent. But, Amanda, have you considered all the ramifications of this thing? If you bring the earl up to scratch, get him to make an offer for you, and then you refuse him, he will surely suffer. Do you want to do that to a man who has never harmed you?"

Tears stood in Amanda's blue eyes. "I don't want to hurt anyone, truly I don't, milady. But I have tried everything I can think of." She sniffled. "Overton simply will not notice me as a woman. He always treats me like I'm a child, and a troublesome child, at that. So I thought—"

Psyche nodded. "Of course. I understand. You thought that having the best catch in London offer for you would show Overton your true worth."

Amanda leaned forward. "Oh yes! Please, milady, help me. I love my guardian so much. I cannot marry anyone else."

Psyche smiled reassuringly. "Don't worry," she said, patting Amanda's hand. "We will contrive it somehow. Just let me think on it for a while."

Some time later Psyche descended the staircase again. Imagine Overton not knowing that Amanda cared for him! But then, her cousin had never struck her as being particularly knowing about women, in spite of his pride in being a fashionable buck. So much of what the young bucks affected was just that — affectation.

But how was she to convince the man that he ought to marry his ward himself? This would take some heavy thinking. And for her, thinking demanded fresh air. She turned toward the front door.

"Lady Psyche," the earl called, appearing in the library doorway, and looking in his usual tip-top form. "Good morning. I see you are up and about. Are you sure you're completely recovered?"

"Quite sure," she returned. "I was just going to take a walk. I find I need a breath of fresh air."

He nodded, his expression grave. "Yes, I was thinking the same thing myself. If you don't mind, I shall accompany you."

"I don't mind," she said, swallowing her smile. No woman with any sense would mind the earl's company!

In a moment he joined her. "So," he said when they had stepped out into the sunshine. "You will soon be in London."

"Yes. London." It was then that she realized. If she had been right, if his attentions to *her* meant he was interested in Amanda, he was going to be disappointed. She didn't want him to be disappointed, but she didn't want him to marry Amanda either.

The earl offered her his arm. "The path may be a little rough. And your recent injury—"

She took his arm, his strong arm. She took it happily. "Thank you. You're very kind."

He raised an eyebrow. "You said that last night."

The thought of last night, of him leaning over her, brought the heat to her cheeks. "I only said what was true."

"You said something else, yesterday, something I didn't quite understand."

She turned to look at him. "And what was that?"

"When I first carried you to the library, you insisted that I put you down. You said you would explain later."

She'd almost forgotten that. "I did?"

"You did." He smiled. "And now I would like my explanation."

"I— I will tell you, but first, milord, I must ask you a rather personal question."

The earl raised an eyebrow, but he simply said, "Ask it then."

"Do you plan to marry soon?"

He almost stopped walking. What a question!

She had effrontery, his Psyche. He wished he could crush her to him, right there, kiss her and tell her *Yes, darling, to you.* Instead he raised an eyebrow. "Marry? Me? I hardly think so."

"Then— Then you don't plan to ask for Amanda's hand?"

Her lower lip quivered slightly. So that was what she thought! Trust Psyche to give him a shocker. He let his face register amazement. "I? Marry that child? Of course not." He frowned. "Why do you ask such a thing?"

Psyche smiled. "I have an idea—about Amanda's future husband. I hope to get her married to a really good man who she can love."

Well, that was a relief. "I'm glad to hear it. Tell me, who is this paragon of virtue?"

Psyche hesitated. "I would tell you, Southdon, but the secret is not mine to divulge. You'll be in London for the Season, though, won't you?"

As if he would miss it! He wanted to see Lady Bluestocking in action. And he intended to change her opinion on marriage. "Of course."

"If Amanda gives me permission—as I think she will—I will tell you then. Indeed, you may be able to help us."

He would do anything for her, but he could hardly say so. "Help you? I'm sure I don't know how." He squeezed the warm fingers that lay upon his sleeve. "But you have certainly piqued my curiosity. And in any case, I would not have missed the return to the ton of Lady Bluestocking. The fireworks should be stupendous."

She frowned. "There will be more than fireworks if those awful Lindens don't stop spreading tales about me."

The earl grinned. "I wouldn't fret. I have every confidence that Lady Bluestocking will get the best of them. And anyone else who gets in her way."

Chapter Nine

Two weeks later Psyche was installed in Overton's town house on Grosvenor Square. Before she'd left the house party, her cousin had faithfully promised to inform his mama that he had asked Psyche to manage Amanda's come-out. But Psyche had arrived in London to find Aunt Anna laboring under the delusion, obviously fostered by that coward Overton, that her niece had come to town merely "to help."

She'd given him a good scold, of course, but she had also commiserated with him. A mama like Aunt Anna, as Psyche well knew, could be a difficult cross to bear. Besides, it didn't matter so terribly much. Since Amanda wished to marry Overton, her come-out would not have to be perfect.

On the other hand, Psyche told herself as she climbed into the carriage one afternoon for a shopping excursion on Bond Street, considering Overton's fastidiousness about propriety, and the fact that he had no knowledge of Amanda's feelings for him, her come-out had better go reasonably well.

To that end they were on their way to the dressmaker. As Psyche had told Georgie only the day before, she would have much preferred to leave Aunt Anna at home, very, very much, but of course her aunt would not hear of such a thing.

Psyche sighed. Georgie had laughed when she'd discovered that so far Psyche had battled with Aunt Anna over the decorations, the music, the food, and the guest list. And unless Psyche changed her tactics as Georgie had suggested, they would no doubt also battle over Amanda's gown.

Still, Psyche could not feel entirely downhearted. The amazing disclosure that Amanda did not nurse a tendre for the earl had raised Psyche's spirits immensely. Even Overton's cowardice and the interminable battles with Aunt Anna could not dampen such good spirits, especially when Psyche considered that the earl would soon arrive in town.

And when he did, she had Amanda's permission to divulge the name of the true object of her affections. Psyche was confident the earl would help them. Somehow, some way, they would make Overton recognize that his feelings for Amanda were rather more than those of a guardian for his ward.

The carriage stopped outside the modiste's establishment. With exaggerated sighs and exclamations, Aunt Anna descended, fluttering her ruffles of muddy-brown sarcenet. For the hundredth time Psyche asked herself why a woman of Aunt Anna's abundant proportions insisted on wearing such an unflattering style. Psyche had, of course, no answer to her question. Perhaps there was none. Perhaps with Aunt Anna, as with Mama, a reason was not necessary.

All London knew the Harley sisters had done as they pleased. The ton gaped, it snickered, it whispered behind its hands, but it did not give the cut direct. The Harley sisters, whatever their idiosyncrasies, were of good blood, moneyed blood. And that sufficed.

With an appealing look to Psyche, Amanda descended from the carriage. Psyche followed. Amanda had shown admirable restraint during Aunt Anna's various fits of fancy. But early this morning the poor girl had come to Psyche's room in tears. "Please, *please*," she begged, "say I may *not* have ruffles on the gown for my come-out."

Psyche had looked up from a letter to her steward and raised an eyebrow. "Ruffles? Why on earth should you have ruffles?"

Amanda sniffled. "Perhaps you haven't noticed, but Aunt Anna is excessively fond of ruffles. And I, I have not the figure to carry them."

Neither did Aunt Anna, but Psyche didn't say so. "Don't worry," she assured Amanda. "There will be no ruffles on your new gown. Trust me. I will see to it."

Amanda smiled in relief. "Thank you, milady. You are very kind to me. I don't know what I would have done without you."

Psyche didn't know either. "Leave it to me," she said. "I will deal with Aunt Anna."

And now the time for dealing had come.

The modiste welcomed them and ushered them into her private room where she indicated a sofa. "If milady would care to sit, I will have the pattern books brought in."

Aunt Anna settled on the sofa and motioned to Amanda to sit beside her. Sending Psyche an imploring glance, Amanda obeyed. A shop girl put a pattern book in her hands and Aunt Anna immediately took it from her and pored over it.

"Now," the modiste said, smiling. "First we decide on the pattern, then we pick the material. I have some excellent new fabrics, very fine, just the thing for a come-out."

Psyche nodded, but Aunt Anna, engrossed in the pattern book, merely grunted.

Psyche smiled at the modiste. "I should like to see a book, too. I shall be needing a gown."

"Of course, milady."

Five minutes later Psyche saw the pattern for a gown that would suit Amanda exquisitely, a simple style in pearl silk, girlish and yet grown-up, and without a single ruffle. She marked the place with her thumb and then started looking for a gown for herself.

Ten minutes later she had found it. She would have it made in claret satin, with a small train, a sophisticated gown for an older woman.

"Amanda," she called. "Come see what you

think of this gown for me."

Amanda came eagerly, leaning to look. "Oh, yes, that will be beautiful."

With a quick glance to be sure Aunt Anna wasn't watching, Psyche opened the book to the other gown. When she raised a questioning eyebrow, Amanda gave her a quick, emphatic nod, her smile brilliant. Psyche patted her hand and gestured her back to the sofa. Perhaps Georgie had been right. Perhaps the best thing was to let Aunt Anna think she'd had her way. And then do as they pleased.

"Have you no patterns with ruffles?" Aunt Anna demanded querulously.

The modiste looked a trifle shocked, but recovered enough to say, "Ruffles are not *in* this Season, milady."

"No matter." Aunt Anna lumbered to her feet and crossed to the stacked bolts of material. "We shall still have a gown with plenty of ruffles. And make it of this." She put her hand on a bolt of bright persimmon silk.

The modiste glanced at Psyche, swallowing hard. "Milady, if I might suggest, that shade doesn't do justice to your color—"

"Oh, it's not for me," Aunt Anna pronounced grandly, waving an impatient hand. "It's for Amanda here. For her come-out."

The modiste looked about to collapse. Of course she recognized the total impropriety of a girl Amanda's age wearing orange to her comeout! While the modiste was trying to rally herself, to find a tactful way to reply, Psyche stepped into the breach. "Aunt Anna, do you think Amanda is looking a little pale?"

Amanda obligingly slumped, clearly doing her best to look ill.

"Perhaps you ought to take her out to the carriage," Psyche suggested. "Get her into the fresh air. I can finish up here."

"Of course," Aunt Anna said, bustling toward the door, and shooing Amanda before her. "Shopping can be so dreadfully tiring. But we have ordered the right gown now. Remember, it must have plenty of ruffles."

As the door closed behind them, the modiste regained her voice. "Milady, surely— We can not— An orange gown— Ruffles—"

"Never mind," Psyche said reassuringly. "It will be all right. Now, here's what I want you to do."

The next afternoon Psyche and Amanda were at their needlepoint in the drawing room while Aunt Anna took her usual afternoon nap. The sound of a carriage halting outside the partially opened window brought Amanda quickly to her feet. She hurried to peer out between the lacy panels.

"Who is it?" Psyche inquired casually, picking out a stitch which had gone astray.

Amanda turned from the window, her face pale. "It's him, milady, it's the earl! Oh, do you really think he'll help us?" She clasped her hands piteously. "Oh do remember, he must promise not to breathe a word to Overton. If my guardian ever finds out, oh, I should die of shame!"

"It will be all right," Psyche said in soothing tones. "When the earl comes in, you can explain—"

"Oh, no! Never! I couldn't—" And Amanda bolted from the room.

Psyche swallowed a sigh. How was she ever to bring together two such pea brains as Amanda and Overton, when neither of them seemed to have the sense he was born with?

"The Earl of Southdon," the butler announced in sonorous tones.

Psyche smiled. "Do come in, Southdon. And sit down."

The earl advanced and bowed before her. "It's good to see you again," he said.

Good? he thought. It was wonderful. He had missed her so very much, as though she'd already become a part of his life. But then, she had. His Psyche, his "soul." The meaning of her Greek name was so appropriate. Long ago, during those lonely nights in Spain she had taken shape in his heart, inhabited a special place there, and without her even knowing it.

He smiled at her, trying not to let her see how much he wished to gather her in his arms, to crush her to him. He swallowed hastily. He must stop this kind of thinking. "You're looking quite well," he said, "considering."

Psyche's welcoming smile turned to a frown of

bewilderment. "Considering what?" she inquired.

The earl settled into the chair Amanda had vacated. Stretching his long legs before him, he leaned back and smiled. "Considering your recurring battles with Overton's mother. I understand there have been disputes over the decorations, the music, the food, the guest—"

"Stop!" Psyche cried, laughter in her beautiful melodious voice. "I didn't know Overton was reporting all this to you." She frowned in obvious puzzlement. "Though I wonder how he even knows. The man has hardly showed his face around here."

The earl removed an almost invisible piece of lint from his sleeve. "It was not Overton who told me your tale of woe. It was Georgie."

"Georgie," Psyche repeated, her voice changing. "You have seen Georgie?"

"But of course." He inspected his cuff. Georgie was right. This was the way to do it. Make Psyche jealous. "We are old friends, Georgie and I. We share everything."

"I see." Psyche managed a smile, at least she hoped it was a smile. "And how did you find Georgie?"

The earl grinned. "In capital spirits, as always. You know Georgie."

Psyche nodded. She was being ridiculous, allowing herself to be upset because he was friendly with Georgie. Still, she couldn't help it, she felt intense disappointment. "It was kind of you to take the time to call," she said primly. "Aunt

Anna will be sorry she missed you. She usually takes a nap at this hour."

"I know."

The frankness of his reply left her flustered. "And Amanda, she, well, I'm afraid this whole thing has been rather difficult for her."

"Quite so," agreed the earl, regarding her steadily.

Psyche picked up her stitching again. It was disconcerting to have him sitting there, staring at her like that. She needed something to occupy her hands.

Several minutes passed in silence. For Psyche they were very long minutes, during which she more than once pricked herself and found it impossible to keep her attention on her embroidery.

Finally the earl said, "I am waiting."

Startled, she raised her gaze from her stitching. "Waiting for what?"

"For the explanation that was promised me."

"Oh, that." Now that the moment was upon her she was ill at ease. In the privacy of her room she had imagined that enlisting his help would be a simple matter, but faced with his presence, his overwhelming presence, she found herself practically tongue-tied. "I do not— It's a very delicate matter— I just don't know—"

"Perhaps," the earl suggested, "you could start by naming the object of Amanda's affection."

Psyche nodded, clutching her embroidery. "Yes, of course. But you must promise not to breathe a word to anyone. It's—" She looked toward the door, lowering her voice. "It's Overton."

Shock registered on the earl's handsome face, then amusement. "Capital!" he cried. "They suit each other admirably."

Psyche sighed. "Do lower your voice. It is not quite so simple."

The earl leaned forward. "You mean there's a fly in the matrimonial buttermilk?"

Psyche nodded. "Very much so."

The earl stroked his chin. "But it seems so simple. Amanda has her come-out, her hour of glory, and then he marries her. What could possibly cause problems?"

Psyche sighed ruefully. "Well there is one, just one, little problem with that lovely progression of events."

"And that is?"

"Overton has shown no interest in marrying her."

The earl raised an eyebrow. "You mean—"

"I mean that Amanda has formed a deep attachment for the man. In fact"—she leaned toward him—"Amanda vows she will marry no other. But in spite of her approaching come-out, Overton persists in regarding her as a child." Psyche shrugged. "And so we have come to a standstill."

The earl frowned thoughtfully. "A terrible pickle if ever I've seen one. But how did you suppose that I could help?"

"Well, you didn't know it, but Amanda had a plan to get Overton to notice her."

The earl looked puzzled. "Of course I didn't know it. Why should I?"

She sighed. "Because it had to do with you."

"Me?" He was sitting erect now, looking quite puzzled. "How me?"

"Amanda planned to get you to offer for her and then to refuse you."

The earl stared at her. Were they both crazy? He hadn't been puffing himself to Psyche. There was hardly a woman in London who would refuse him. Except Lady Bluestocking. "Refuse me?" he repeated.

Psyche nodded. "I'm afraid Amanda is rather naive, but her reasoning was sound. She has been told that you are the best catch of the Season. And she thought that your offering for her would make her guardian sit up and take notice."

The earl stroked his chin again. "It's not a bad plan, but it's impossible, of course. No one who knows me would believe I'd offer for such a child."

He smiled at her warmly. He was supposed to make Psyche jealous. At least, Georgie had said he should. This whole plan was her idea, her female idea. He would have preferred a straightforward approach, a frontal attack, so to speak. But he'd begun this way, so he'd better go on. "It's well known among the ton that I prefer experienced women."

Experienced women like Georgie. Psyche pushed the thought aside. Aloud she said, "Of course. I pointed out to her that the thing

110

wouldn't work." She sighed. "I had hoped that once we were in town I could throw the two of them together. But Overton is always out somewhere. We see him only in passing."

The earl crossed his legs, idly swinging his booted foot. Psyche's mind presented her with the memory of the ruined abbey and the seat of the earl's breeches. Heat rose to her cheeks and she resumed her stitching, but that was no help either and finally, unable to bear the silence any longer, she looked up again. "Have you any suggestions?"

For some moments longer the earl sat, considering the toe of his shining boot, and then his frown smoothed out. "Perhaps I can help."

Psyche dropped her needlework. "Oh, thank you, we shall be eternally grateful!"

He smiled and raised an eyebrow. "Perhaps you'd better wait to see what results we get."

He leaned forward, gazing into Psyche's eyes. For a moment she forgot everything except his overwhelming nearness. Then she regained a little sense. "What?" she whispered. "What is your plan?"

He smiled. "Actually it is your plan. I mean only to implement it. I won't actually court the child, but I may drop a few hints, see if I can open your cousin's eyes—"

"You promised." Psyche leaned forward and clutched his arm. "You must not tell him—"

The earl's hand covered hers, such a warm hand, so strong. "Don't worry," he said lightly. "I

111

will handle it all. But you must forewarn Amanda. After the come-out, I shall contrive some occasions to throw them together. Some excursions to see the city, perhaps. You and I will go along, of course."

Her heart rose up in her throat, making further thanks difficult to utter.

He looked at his pocket watch. "Now, I'm afraid I must go. I'll be out of town for a few days, necessary estate business, but I'll see you at the come-out."

Chapter Ten

The days passed. In spite of the frenzied activity, the fitting of gowns, the ordering of flowers and food, the constant coming and going of tradespeople, all the continual rush and stir of preparation, Psyche found the days endless.

The earl was still out of town. He would not return until the very day of Amanda's come-out. And so for Psyche, though she filled them with activities too numerous to count, the days dragged slowly by.

But finally the day of the come-out arrived. Feeling as nervous as if the great event had been designed in *her* honor, Psyche had her claret gown laid out, all its accoutrements ready, and had set Curtis to dressing her hair, when the door burst open and Amanda came flying in, tears streaming down her face.

"Psyche!" she wailed. "Will you look at me! Just look at me! I'm a sight! I cannot bear it! Why, why, I would frighten little children! Set them to screaming, I'm sure!"

Psyche looked. And looked again. Unfortunately, Amanda was right. Arrayed in the gown of ruffled persimmon silk, the poor girl rather resembled a fat, fluttering squash. Psyche bit her bottom lip, with great difficulty keeping a sober face. She didn't want to laugh when poor Amanda was already distraught. And no wonder.

"Oh, God!" Amanda moaned. "This is horrible. If Overton sees me like this, I shall die!"

"Steady," Psyche soothed, rising to her feet and crossing to Amanda's side. "He's not at home yet. And no one else will see you. Remember, we have the plan."

"I know, I know." Amanda nodded bravely, but then she peered down at her gown, and her face took on an expression of utter horror. "Oh dear, can't we go ahead and do it now?"

Psyche looked at the clock. "No, dear. It's simply too early. I promise you, though, when the time comes, you will be stunning." She squeezed her hand. "Now, chin up. And remember, don't let on to anything in front of Aunt Anna."

Amanda straightened her shoulders. "I won't." She gave Psyche a tremulous sigh and marched out, looking for all the world like she was headed for her own execution.

"Lord love a duck!" Curtis exclaimed when the door was safely shut. "That old lady has got

114

to be missing something upstairs. I ain't never seen such a horrendous gown! How could anyone buy such a thing on purpose?"

Psyche smiled and settled again at her dressing table. "Wait till you see Aunt Anna's gown. It's the most bilious green, like—like pond scum."

Curtis shuddered. "The poor young lady! She must love Lord Overton a lot to take on such an awful woman as his mama." Curtis grinned at her in the mirror, fussing with a curl. "But she'll learn how to get on from you, milady. You always managed your mama real good. This plan of your'n, it'll work, too."

Psyche grinned back. She and Curtis had long been friends. "I just hope Amanda doesn't get impatient and rush things." She glanced at the clock again. "It's good we'll have my hair done—so you'll be free to help her."

When there remained but half an hour till the guests were expected, Psyche and Curtis exchanged glances. Before they could look away, a piercing scream echoed through the upper reaches of the house. "Right on time," Psyche said, grinning. Then, clad in her wrapper, she raced down the hall.

Aunt Anna blocked the door to Amanda's room. She stood aghast, one large hand at her open mouth, the other clutching the door frame. "Oh no! Amanda! Your beautiful gown!"

With her aunt's shrieks threatening to split her eardrums, Psyche pushed past her into the room. Amanda stood in the middle of the floor, still swathed in persimmon silk. But down the gown's front, and spreading across its ruffled layers, ran a series of ink spots.

Psyche swallowed a smile. Amanda had followed instructions to perfection. The ink blots were large and prominently placed. There was no way on earth to disguise them. And no time to even try to remove them.

"Oh dear! Oh dear!" Aunt Anna wailed, frantically wringing her hands. "What shall we do? You can't appear in public all spotted with ink like that." She frowned. "And why on earth were you writing in your new gown?"

Amanda's lower lip trembled and a big tear slipped down her cheek. "I'm sorry. I— I just wished to record my thoughts about this happy day."

"Well, you have quite ruined your lovely gown," Aunt Anna lamented. "I'm sure you didn't mean to, but I just don't know what we can do! It will all be spoiled, ruined. The whole come-out. All the flowers and food. We'll have to call it—"

Psyche crossed the room. "Dear Aunt Anna. Do calm down. Perhaps I can help. I have in my armoire a gown that might fit Amanda."

Aunt Anna sighed piteously and wrung her hands. "But you're much taller than she."

"Yes, I know. That's why I haven't worn the gown. It was too short for me. But I just didn't get around to taking it to the dressmaker to be fixed."

Aunt Anna exhaled loudly. "Well, I suppose it will have to do. Such a shame, that beautiful, beautiful gown. All those lovely ruffles."

Putting both hands to her temples, she backed out of the door. "I'm afraid you'll have to take care of it, Psyche. This is just too much for my poor, poor nerves."

"Of course, Aunt Anna," Psyche soothed. "You just go get dressed. Amanda, you come with me."

The gown of pearl silk fit Amanda to perfection, but of course they knew it would since she'd secretly tried it on right after it had arrived. Its high-waisted bodice fit snugly and the skirt fell gracefully to the floor. In it she looked as a young woman at her come-out was meant to look, sweet and innocent, and yet a woman.

Her face radiant, Amanda twirled before the cheval glass. "Oh, Psyche, it's beautiful. I look so grown-up. Do you think he'll notice me?"

Psyche sighed. She hoped so. She wished so. But with Overton she couldn't be sure. "We'll just have to wait and see. But you are so beautiful. I'm sure other men will notice you. And you must laugh and speak with them. Perhaps flirt a little."

Amanda started to pout. "I don't want—"

117

"You listen to Lady Psyche," Curtis said, reaching out to adjust a blond curl on the top of Amanda's head. "She knows what she's about."

Amanda gave her a sidelong look. "But— But *she* didn't catch a husband. So how does she know—"

Curtis gave an exasperated groan. "Girl, where's your brains? She didn't get a husband 'cause she didn't *want* a husband. Were she wanting a husband, why, she'd go right out and find herself one. Just like that."

Hastily, Psyche turned away. Curtis had been in on her Lady Bluestocking exploits, had even helped her think them up. Curtis's faith in her was heartening. It was also misplaced. Because, Psyche thought, if she'd had the least idea how to get a man to propose marriage, she would have gotten herself such a proposal from the earl long before this.

The clock chimed the hour and Psyche's heart thudded. Soon now. Soon the earl would be arriving.

Minutes later Psyche looked around the ballroom. The flowers were excessive and on the large side, but at least they weren't orange. And getting them properly arranged had kept Aunt Anna so occupied that she would not immediately notice that there had been a slight—or rather a considerable—change in the menu. The six different flavors of ices her aunt had wanted were definitely excessive. The present repast would be quite sufficient—and not cause a lot of unfavorable talk.

Cook had been quite amenable after Overton had spoken to her. So had the footmen, who had conveniently neglected to deliver invitations to certain unsavory people Aunt Anna had meant to include. Everyone in the house, with the exception of Aunt Anna herself, knew that Psyche was managing the come-out, and all acted accordingly.

Psyche surveyed the ballroom with a sense of satisfied accomplishment. Considering all they had gone through, all the trouble and worry, things were going quite well.

Aunt Anna came bustling up, a massive figure in sickly green ruffles. She patted her frizzled hair and surveyed Amanda's gown critically through her quizzing glass. "Well, I suppose it will have to do. But it's dreadfully plain, no ruffles at all. In my day a well-dressed young woman always wore ruffles. Your mama and I both knew that."

Since her own mama had hated ruffles, never permitting them on any of her numerous gowns, Psyche found Aunt Anna's pronouncement rather difficult to believe. But she nodded. "Yes, Aunt Anna. Of course, Aunt Anna."

Aunt Anna adjusted the ruffle that hung from

her bodice. "Yes, well. Too bad. But we'd better form the receiving line. The guests will be arriving soon."

She pressed a pudgy hand to her forehead. "Now, where is that boy of mine? Overton ought to be here."

"I am here, Mama." Overton appeared behind her. "Right here." He turned to Psyche. "Is everything in order?"

"Of course," Aunt Anna replied, just as though he had spoken to her. "You know what a good manager I am. I'm just sorry Amanda ruined her gown. It was quite an expensive gown and —"

"Of orange silk," Psyche said softly.

"With lots of ruffles," Amanda added.

Overton's face began to turn pink. "Orange?" He pulled at his cravat. "Ruffles?"

"Indeed," Psyche continued. "It was a very unique gown."

Her cousin looked about to succumb to apoplexy.

"But unfortunately," Psyche hastened to add, "Amanda was writing in her diary and spilled some ink on her gown, making it unfit to wear."

Recognition and relief mingled on Overton's face, and his color slowly returned to normal.

"But," Psyche went on, "I happened to have a new gown in my armoire. And it fit Amanda to perfection. Doesn't she look lovely in it?"

Amanda flushed a deep pink as Overton looked her over. "Very pretty," he said, nodding, "very pretty. She looks nice in anything, of course. But what is this about—"

"Overton," Psyche interrupted. "May I speak to you for a moment privately?"

When she got him aside, out of his mother's hearing, she spoke to him quite frankly. "The gown Amanda is wearing was made especially for her. But to avoid argument I let Aunt Anna think it was mine and we purchased the orange silk that she wanted."

Overton raised an eyebrow and tugged at his cravat. "And the accident with the ink?"

Psyche smiled. "A fortuitous event."

"Quite fortuitous," Overton exclaimed. "My God, how the ton would have talked if she'd appeared in orange ruffles! I owe you for that, Psyche." He shuddered. "Orange ruffles! Of all the addle-brained schemes!"

"You must not let on," Psyche said, "to your mama that the accident was not really—"

Overton drew himself up. "Of course not. I'm not a pea brain." He turned. "Come, we'd better get back. I want to see who appeals to Amanda. Her husband has to be a special fellow, you know."

Psyche followed him to the receiving line.

She'd barely taken her place there when Georgie came in on Gresham's arm. Seeing her, Psyche swallowed a sigh of relief. Georgie

121

hadn't come with the earl, so perhaps he would come alone. Maybe he would even ask Psyche for a waltz. It was a pleasant prospect, the thought of whirling around the floor in the earl's arms, very pleasant. But this was Amanda's party. She had to think about Amanda.

Visitor after visitor arrived, filling the ballroom with their bright chatter and the tinkle of laughter. Finally Aunt Anna allowed the receiving line to dissolve and the music began.

In a chair beneath some palms, Psyche settled to watch the dancers. So young they looked, so vibrant and full of life.

She smoothed the claret silk of her skirt. Where was *he?* Why hadn't the earl arrived?

She swallowed a sigh. What did it matter? If he had arrived, he would be dancing with Georgie. She was out on the floor this very minute, whirling in the steps of the waltz, and smiling up at every man within smiling distance.

Georgie was beautiful, vivacious tonight in a gown of sea-foam green embroidered with seed pearls, her face bright with laughter, her eyes shining with enjoyment.

Lucky Georgie to be able to delight in the presence of so many men. Psyche sighed again. There was only one man who could make *her* glow like that, one man whose attentions meant more to her than she knew how to say. But the earl only saw her as someone to banter with, someone safe who would not try to trap him into a marriage he didn't want.

Well, Psyche thought crossly as the dancers twirled by, he needn't worry about that. She couldn't trap him if she tried. She simply didn't know how.

"You are pensive tonight," the earl said, emerging from beside the palms. "How are things going?"

Psyche swallowed hard, trying to stop the foolish grin of joy that had risen to her face at the sight of him. "All things considered, I think the come-out is going well. We managed to eliminate the orange flowers—and the orange gown."

The earl raised an eyebrow. "Are you telling me—"

Psyche smiled. "My aunt insisted on buying Amanda an orange gown." She paused. "A ruffled orange gown."

"Good God! Where is the poor child?"

"There's no need to worry," Psyche said. "Amanda spilled ink on her gown at the last minute. And so she was forced to wear one of mine."

"Ah ha!" He raised the other eyebrow, looking her up and down. "And I suppose you are going to tell me that it fit her perfectly despite the difference in your heights."

Psyche nodded, unable to hold back a grin. "Just as though it had been made for her."

The earl chuckled. "My dear Lady Bluestocking," he drawled, "it's such a shame you never married."

Psyche's heart rose up in her throat. "Why is that?"

"Because, you are so admirably adept at using devious methods."

What did he mean? She didn't know a thing about being devious. If she had— "Devious methods?" she repeated.

He nodded, his eyes dancing with mischief. "Yes, the kind wives use to get what they want from husbands."

She couldn't help it. She bristled. "Indeed!"

The earl looked amused, his mouth curving into a brash grin. She wished for a moment, childishly, to kick him hard in the shins, but of course she couldn't. Such behavior was most unladylike. "And why is it that wives must stoop to using devious means to get what they need from husbands?" she inquired caustically.

"I'm sure I don't know," he said, "never having had a wife."

Psyche gave him a cold look. "That's true," she said, "and very fortunate, too, considering your attitude."

He surveyed her with lazy, laughing eyes. She wanted to be angry, she *was* angry, but she was so glad to see him. And he looked marvelous. So big and strong and handsome. No wonder women threw themselves into his arms.

She sighed in exasperation. She wanted him to

think of her in wifely terms — and here she was, doing and saying all the wrong things. Being Lady Bluestocking again.

The earl raised a hand, as though he meant to ward off a blow. "I beg your pardon," he said. "I didn't mean to conjure up Lady Bluestocking." She frowned at him, but he forged on. "I'm afraid you won't appreciate my saying it, but you are very lovely when you're angry."

He didn't know what was driving him to provoke her. He ought to be smoothing her feathers, not ruffling them. But somehow he wanted to see Lady Bluestocking with his own eyes, see her come flaming to the defense of womankind. And she was magnificent, her eyes blazing, her chin thrust stubbornly out, defending her sex against all comers.

"If the world were run on equality," she pointed out crisply, "there would be little need for deception. But since women are the weaker sex — not in intellect, but in power and physical prowess — they must use whatever they can to achieve their ends."

He liked the fierce way she glared at him. His Psyche was no milksop, no simpering maiden always bowing to his wishes. She would be herself — the self he loved.

But did she really believe what she'd said? He fixed her with a hard look. "Are you telling me that the end justifies the means?"

Psyche hesitated. She didn't really believe

that. She couldn't. But what she had said did sound like it. "I— No, I don't believe that, but—"

He rose to his feet, looking so handsome in his black evening clothes that her heart began to thud painfully again.

He turned to her. "I suppose I shall have to do this the conventional way." He bowed over her hand. "Would you honor me with this dance?"

"I— Should I—"

"Amanda certainly is well taken care of," he pointed out. "You may have one dance to yourself."

Psyche managed to pull herself together. "It is kind of you to ask me, but—"

He took a step closer. "Kindness has absolutely nothing to do with it," he replied with that lazy grin. "I *wish* to dance with you. Now *you* can be kind and consent."

He extended a hand and waited expectantly, smiling down on her.

Psyche surrendered to her feelings and got to her feet. "Very well," she said, trying not to smile in such a giddy fashion. "One dance. But then we must find Overton and do what we can to help Amanda."

126

Chapter Eleven

One dance, and only one dance. That was what Psyche told herself when she let the earl lead her to the dance floor. He took her right hand in his left, put his other hand in the small of her back. Her gown of claret silk was quite heavy and of course he was wearing gloves, but she could feel his hand burning through the material, almost scorching her skin.

"I—" She hesitated. "I have not learned to waltz," she murmured. "When I had my Season, the waltz was not yet—"

"There is nothing to it," he interrupted cheerfully, with that grin that made her heart turn over. "It's just a one-two-three thing." He smiled. "Put yourself in my hands and I will guide you." He looked down at her and chuckled. "That is, if Lady Bluestocking will *allow* a man to guide her."

The touch of his hand had made her so giddy she could not think how to reply, had to concentrate instead on not melting into him.

When she didn't answer, he raised an eyebrow. "Perhaps you will permit me to point out that, though a lady may not need a man to manage her estate any more than a fish may need wings to swim, a lady *may* find a man useful *if* she wishes to waltz."

"Yes," Psyche conceded with a smile, at last finding her tongue. "You are right. I will do as you say and allow you to guide me — through the waltz." She would allow him to guide her through life, through anything, she thought, but there was no way to let him know that.

"Now," he went on, in that lazy drawl that somehow made her remember quite vividly the feel of being carried in his arms. "This is how we do it. Lean back against my hand. And give yourself up entirely to the music. Can you do that?"

"Yes," Psyche said.

And they were off, whirling around the floor in intoxicating circles. He clasped her so close she inhaled the tang of leather, of spice. She felt the comforting, almost possessive, pressure of his hand on her back. Closing her eyes, she gave herself completely up to him.

The music ebbed and swelled around them, its wonderful beat invading her body, setting her heart to thumping in rhythm with it. It was mad, it was glorious, it was like nothing she'd ever felt before. No wonder Lord Byron had called the waltz wanton. No wonder he felt it heated a man's blood. A woman's, too, though probably few ladies would have admitted it.

All too soon the music stopped. And they stopped dancing. Reluctantly, Psyche stepped back, out of the earl's arm. "Thank you. That was most enjoyable."

His eyes were so warm she thought they might burn a hole right through her. "For me, too," he said, his voice low. "I wish—"

"There you are!" Miss Linden paused beside them, watery blue eyes gleaming. "Milord, how good to see you. And you, Lady Psyche." She gave Psyche's gown a quick appraisal. "Claret is not really your color, but otherwise that gown is quite nice."

"Thank you," Psyche murmured, her expression blank.

The earl kept a tight hold on the fingers that trembled in his. Psyche was upset, he thought, but her face wasn't showing it.

Miss Linden inched closer, blinking up into his eyes. What did this whey-faced creature expect from him? He certainly did not mean to dance with her. He wanted only to dance with Psyche. All night with Psyche. Forever with Psyche.

And then it came to him, the Linden chit could be useful. Keeping a tight hold on Psyche's hand, he gave Miss Linden his finest smile. "If you'll excuse us, I believe this is our dance." And he whirled Psyche away.

She was silent for several minutes and then she looked up at him, and never missing a beat asked, "Really, Southdon, why have you done such a foolish thing?"

He made his voice serious and pretended surprise. "Of what sin am I to be convicted now?"

"You know you have danced with me twice," she pointed out, frowning at him. "Twice, and in a row. People will talk."

He raised a nonchalant eyebrow. "Have you forgotten that you are Lady Bluestocking?"

Perplexed, she stared up at him. "Of course not. All London knows that."

"And all London also knows that you have no use for marriage—or men. So they will think nothing of another dance with me. A slight idiosyncrasy on your part, nothing more."

She ought to refute his illogic. She knew it. But she was too conscious of his nearness to step out of his arms, too full of longing for his touch to forfeit even one sweet second of this dance.

"Very well," she said. "But as you well know, this must be our last dance. Then we must attend to Overton."

The earl nodded gravely. "As always, your wish is my command. And by the way, claret *is* your color."

They left the dance floor at the end of the waltz, the earl tucking her arm through his as though it were the most natural thing in the world.

She let her arm stay there, let her hand rest upon his warm sleeve. She did this only, she told herself fighting a certain lightheadedness, because he was going to talk to Overton. And of course, as he had so aptly pointed out before, he could be seen in Lady Bluestocking's company with complete safety. No one would ever expect him to marry *her.*

That was not the happiest thought and she pushed it aside. Tonight she must think about Amanda, only about Amanda. "Do be careful," she whispered, glancing up at the earl. "We don't want Overton to suspect—"

The earl frowned, but his eyes were twinkling, dancing with mischief, in fact. "I say, Lady Bluestocking, do you doubt my capacity for deception?"

"I—" That was not a conversation she wished to resume. "I just want you to be careful. If Overton finds out, Amanda will be devastated."

The earl smiled. "Cupid's arrow has struck deep then."

"Indeed, yes," Psyche agreed. "Unrequited love is such an uncomfortable bedfellow."

The earl sent her a strange look. "A peculiar sentiment for Lady Bluestocking, is it not? I'd have thought she'd have more caustic words for love. Unrequited or otherwise."

"I—I only meant that that is what I've heard." She was heartily tired of all this talk of Lady Bluestocking. She opened her mouth to tell him so—and closed it again quickly. Saying

131

such a thing might drive him from her side. And she would rather have him with her this way than not at all.

By then they had reached Overton, who was standing alone by some palms, watching the dancers go by. Psyche, following his glance, saw that it was resting on Amanda, an Amanda who gave every appearance of being fascinated with the man in whose arms she went whirling around the floor.

"The evening seems to be going well," the earl commented.

"Yes," agreed Overton, still watching Amanda. "I am pleased." He smiled and for a moment Psyche saw how Amanda could love him. "I suppose Psyche told you about the gown — and the other things."

"Yes," the earl said. "It's fortunate you had her to manage the thing for you."

Overton heaved a great sigh and tugged at his cravat. "I know it. With Mama like she is, it's been the most tremendous job. And I'm eternally grateful to Psyche." He turned. "But tell me, what do you think of Amanda?"

"She's a lovely young woman," the earl said. "She'll make some man a fine wife."

Overton nodded proudly. "Did a good job if I do say so myself. Couldn't have done better."

"Have you someone in mind as her husband?" the earl inquired.

Overton frowned. "No, not really. I want to please her, of course. She's such a delicate-minded little thing. I don't want her to have any of those oafish fellows like Psyche's mama pressed on her. Nor old ones neither. This fellow has to be young and good enough. To take care of Amanda and all."

The earl nodded. "Admirable standards. I quite understand. Have you danced with her yourself yet?"

Overton started, his eyes rounding, his hand reaching for his cravat again. "Gracious, no! You think I should?"

"Of course. It shows your approval."

Overton nodded, his face serious. "Right, I'll do it."

The earl, searching his friend's face, recognized the signs. There was no doubt of it. Overton was snared. Caught good and proper. He just didn't know it yet.

The earl looked down at Psyche. So unrequited love was an uncomfortable bedfellow. Perhaps. But *he* didn't intend to find out. His love would not go unrequited. He meant to make Lady Bluestocking his wife.

Strange, no woman had ever affected him as she did. He'd been on the town five years before he went off to fight Napoleon. And in that time, he'd seen many beautiful women, loved more than a few of them. Or thought so at the time. But those feelings had been but pale imitations of what he felt for Psyche, his Psyche.

The dance ended and Overton went off to claim Amanda for the next one.

"Well, what do you think?" Psyche asked anxiously.

He was tempted to ask her "think about what," but, poor darling, she really was worried about Amanda. "I think he's taken with her."

"Then why doesn't he speak?"

The earl grinned. "The poor fool doesn't know it yet, that's all."

Psyche sighed in exasperation. "How can we make him realize it?" She grimaced. "Short of hitting him over the head with something."

The earl shrugged. "Some men are rather dense in matters of love."

"Indeed!" Psyche snorted. "I should say so."

Her gloved hand lay still upon his coat sleeve. He covered it with his own. "Please, Psyche, don't fret yourself over this. I promise you—we will contrive it someway, somehow. Amanda will have her Overton.

"And now," he said, "how would you like to set this company on its collective ear?"

Psyche stared up into his eyes, eyes dancing with laughter. Why must he be such a terribly attractive man? "And how shall I do that?"

"Simple. Dance with me again."

"Southdon!" Shock had made her voice rise. People nearby turned to look at them. She spoke more softly. "We have already danced twice. You know to do more will cause talk. Why, it might even prevent suitors from calling on Amanda."

"So it might," the earl agreed, raising a mocking eyebrow. "And would that be such a terrible thing, considering that—"

"No, I guess not." Psyche looked out on the dance floor, where an adoring Amanda was being whirled around and gazing up at her guardian from worshipful eyes. "But . . ."

Psyche sighed. She loved the waltz, the invigorating beat, the tantalizing rhythm, the feel of the music in her very blood. But most of all she loved being in the earl's arms, loved the excitement, the joy of it.

"Didn't I do a good job before?" he inquired. "Guiding you through the steps of the dance?"

"Yes," she conceded. "And I admit there's some logic to what you propose, but Southdon— You know how my cousin is about propriety. He will explode when he hears this!"

The earl laughed. "Look at him. He wouldn't notice if everyone else in the room left!" He took a step toward the dance floor. "Come, Lady Bluestocking, I dare you!"

"That's unfair!" she cried, unable to keep from laughing. "To use what I told you about myself against me. How ungentlemanly."

He extended a hand, grinning down at her. "Indeed, it is ungentlemanly. But it's also fun. Come, what do you care? They talked about you before. The whole of fashionable London repeated your epigrams with great glee."

She swallowed a sigh. "I know."

"It didn't bother you then. Don't let it bother you now. Let them talk. We won't mind it."

"You are mad," Psyche said. "No one goes against the dictates of the ton. Lady Jersey and the others—"

"Do you wish to frequent Almack's? Eat stale cake and drink warm lemonade?"

"Of course not. I'm too ol— My Season is over."

"Then you need not fear Almack's patronesses. Do you wish to make calls and be received?"

She glared at him in mock exasperation. "You know I don't. I wish only to get Amanda safely married to Overton."

Again he smiled down into her eyes. "Then dance with me. I will handle anything Overton may say to you. And I will bear the brunt of his criticism."

Psyche laughed. It was not a healthy laugh, but one of resignation. "You will go home," she said. "When the ball is over, you will go home. And I will remain here—with Overton—and bear his scolding."

The earl let his hand fall to his side. "I am sorry," he said. "You are quite right."

Perversely, Psyche wished he hadn't given up. Other women had their husbands, had someone to love them. And she had no one. As soon as Overton could be made to see the truth, she would return to Sussex. But life in the country would never be the same—not after this, not after she knew what it was like to dance with a man she loved, to be carried in his arms, to feel his breath on her cheek, to wish for—

"You are quite right," he said. "I am beyond the bounds on this. We will just watch. Proper, staid, correct."

But she didn't want to be correct. She wanted, desperately, dangerously, to be in his arms again. And this might be her last chance. "Yes," she said.

He raised an eyebrow. "Yes," she repeated more firmly. "We will dance again. But you must help me with Overton when he finds out. You know how he fusses. And we must make him recognize that he loves Amanda."

"Have no fear about that," said the earl. "I have in mind a plan."

Psyche frowned. "If only we could speak outright to him."

The earl shook his head. "I don't think that would work. You must never give Overton advice, at least not openly. You must sneak it in, let him think it is his own idea."

Psyche stared at him. "You speak like someone who knows."

Fool, the earl told himself. *You can't let her know that you planted the idea of her managing Amanda's come-out in her cousin's mind.* He nodded. "Well, he has been my friend for some time. So I've learned how to deal with him." He smiled at her, putting all his charm into it. But still she frowned. Why wouldn't the charm that had put London's women at his feet work on this one who meant so much to him?

He had no answer. But he knew he wouldn't give up. Psyche was meant for him. He didn't question that; he couldn't. He took her in his arms, smiled down into her lovely face, and waltzed her out on the floor.

Chapter Twelve

That dance ended, too, far too soon to suit Psyche. And as they left the dance floor, Georgie approached them, Gresham trailing behind her.

"Southdon!" she cried. "You naughty boy!" She rapped him smartly on the wrist with her fan. "You have been here long enough to dance and you have not come to pay your respects to me. How dare you, you wretch!"

The earl smiled and bowed over her outstretched hand. "A thousand pardons, Georgie dear. But I saw you occupied with Gresham there. And I would never wish to intrude."

Georgie shrugged, as though dismissing the man behind her. "Have you forgotten that you promised me a dance?"

"Of course not. How could I?"

Psyche swallowed a sigh, and watched as Georgie led the earl off.

"Like a tame bear," Gresham murmured.

Psyche turned. Gresham looked as though he'd lost his best friend. "I beg your pardon?"

"She leads a man, any man, around like a tame bear," Gresham explained. He sighed, fixing her with a beseeching look. "You're her friend, Psyche. Tell me, please, how can I win her?"

Psyche bit back brittle laughter. She was hardly the person to give advice in matters of love. But the man was so troubled, she had to do something to help him. "I don't know," she began. "Have you indicated your feelings to her?"

Gresham groaned. "Oh yes, many times. But she laughs at me and then she smiles at someone else." He ran a hand through his hair, leaving it even more mussed than usual. "She treats me like a servant. And yet, sometimes, I think I see in her eyes that, that she may care about me."

He sighed piteously. "It's driving me crazy. *She's* driving me crazy. Oh, Psyche, what am I to do?"

She frowned. "I don't really know, but I have heard—"

"Yes, what?" He stared at her eagerly.

"I have heard that some women, like some men, can be won by making them jealous."

"Jealous?" Gresham considered this. "You mean I should pretend to have a tendre for someone else?"

Psyche nodded. "Perhaps you needn't go quite that far. That is, you don't wish to cause some poor young woman pain."

"Of course not." Gresham's face brightened. "Jealous! Yes! I will try that. And thank you."

"You're quite welcome. I only hope it works."

Psyche watched Gresham stride off to where a

beautiful young thing waited to be swept away in the dance. And she noted that he maneuvered his partner past Georgie and the earl, and that while doing so, Gresham appeared to take no notice of them at all.

Jealousy, Psyche thought, sinking into a chair, was supposed to be a primitive human emotion. Could they use jealousy to bring Overton up to scratch, to get him to offer for Amanda himself? She'd have to ask the earl and see what he thought about it. Too bad she didn't know some way to make *him* jealous.

But even if someone else danced with her, which she doubted would happen given her reputation, the earl would feel no jealousy. He didn't think of her in that way, but merely as a friend, someone safe to talk to. Someone, she thought bitterly, who would not always be throwing herself into his arms.

On the other side of the ballroom, Aunt Anna, like some giant ruffled beast, bore down on Overton. Her fan waved wildly as she gesticulated. And then she held up three gloved fingers.

That was it, Psyche thought, as a scowling Overton glanced her way. The fat was in the fire. Who would have thought that Aunt Anna would be the one to count dances?

Psyche straightened in her chair, bracing herself. Overton was crossing the dance floor toward her, determination in his gaze. From the look of him he didn't mean to wait till the ball was over. She was in for a royal scold. And right now.

She glanced out over the room. Where was the

141

earl when she needed him? And then she spied him, whirling in great circles around the floor, while Georgie laughed up at him, her perfect white teeth sparkling, her pink lips gently parted.

Psyche gnawed on her bottom lip. This was to add insult to injury. Not only must she bear the scolding alone, but while she was doing it the earl would be dancing and flirting with Georgie!

"Psyche!"

Overton stood before her, his face a veritable thundercloud.

She got to her feet. "Yes, cousin?"

"You—! The earl—! How could you?"

She didn't bother to ask him what he was upset about. "We danced," she said calmly. "It meant nothing."

Overton did not look appeased. "Nothing, you say! Three times with the earl! Three times! It's outrageous."

"It's nothing of the sort," Psyche said. "Why make such a fuss over an extra dance?"

Overton frowned. "It's not the dance, but the fact that you defied convention. The patronesses—"

Psyche shrugged. "Some old women. Who gave them the right to make the rules?"

Overton's face slowly turned purple. "Who?" he sputtered.

"Psyche's right."

She turned. The earl stood behind her, Georgie hanging on his arm.

"We give the patronesses too much power," the earl continued with a comforting glance at

Psyche. "We wanted to dance and so we did. Why should we let someone dictate to us?"

"Why indeed?" echoed Georgie, looking up at him with laughing eyes.

Overton frowned. "You're all missing the point. By your selfish behavior you have done irreparable damage to Amanda's reputation." He glared at Psyche. "I am very disappointed in you."

The earl stiffened. This had gone far enough. No one was going to treat his Psyche in this demeaning fashion. "Come now, Overton," he said, putting iron in his voice. "That's enough. None of this was Psyche's fault. It was my idea, all of it."

A flush of color stole slowly up Psyche's cheeks, making her even more beautiful. God, how he wanted to take her in his arms, surround her with his love, keep her safe always.

Let the whole world chatter. They meant nothing to him. No one would hurt his Psyche. He wouldn't let them.

Overton stood silent, but he seemed plainly unconvinced.

"The earl is right," Georgie said, patting his sleeve in a possessive way and smiling at Overton. Unfortunately, since he was watching Overton, he missed Psyche's reaction to Georgie's ploy. "A person should be able to dance with whomever he pleases," she declared.

"Well," Overton conceded, appearing mollified by Georgie's considerable charm. "Perhaps. But Mama was all distraught, making such a row and—"

"Too bad you didn't let your mama manage *tonight*," the earl began pointedly. "Amanda would have been quite striking in that gown of —"

Overton gulped and turned to Psyche. "I'm sorry. I've been unfair to you. You've worked very hard on this come-out." He sighed. "I don't wish to be ungrateful. I know you'll help me find Amanda a proper husband. It's just that sometimes Mama drives me quite mad with her plans and her complaints."

"I understand," Psyche said. And she actually did. She glanced at the earl, who was still wearing Georgie on his sleeve, and then back to Overton. "If you'll excuse me, cousin, I must see to the refreshments."

Overton nodded. "Of course."

"Wait," Georgie called after her. "I will come with you. It's been a while since we had a nice chat."

With the earl looking on, Psyche could only nod.

"The ball is going very well," Georgie said as they moved across the floor. "You have done a really admirable job. I could never have managed such a thing. And to do so with Overton's mama thwarting you at every turn —" She shook her golden head. "I cannot understand how you can bear to be in the same house with such a woman."

Psyche shrugged. "You forget. My own mama gave me a lot of practice."

Frowning, Georgie patted her arm. "You poor dear. Well, once you get Amanda properly married you can return to Sussex." Georgie sent her a sidelong glance. "That is what you mean to do, isn't it?"

Psyche stared straight ahead. "Yes, of course."

"Well, Amanda will have to marry someone other than Southdon. He would not want—"

"Yes," Psyche said, more sharply than she intended. "I know. He would not want such a child."

Georgie nodded and rolled her eyes. "Isn't he a fine figure of a man, though? So handsome, so charming, so—"

"The earl is a man," Psyche said abruptly, "Like any other man."

"Of course." Georgie grinned. "I thought maybe you'd gotten over that Lady Bluestocking nonsense, but I see you haven't. Really, Psyche, I'm worried about you. You need to forget that silliness and find yourself a husband."

"I—I don't wish to talk about it," Psyche said firmly. "And if we're on the subject of possible husbands, why do you treat poor Gresham so abominably? The man really admires you, you know."

Georgie shrugged. "I can't help what men feel for me. And tell me, why should I settle for a viscount when I can have an earl? Oh look, Lady Jersey is motioning to me. I must go."

And she hurried away. A curse rose to Psyche's lips, but she swallowed it. Georgie was Georgie— and there was no point in railing about it. The earl had been on the town for some time. Certainly he was conversant with all the varied traps which a single woman might lay for a man. He would not be caught unless he wished it.

The thought gave her scant comfort. He might well wish it. Georgie was beautiful—and she knew how to give a man what he wanted.

Across the room the earl was still smoothing Overton's ruffled feathers. "You have done an admirable job with Amanda," he said. "Of course, she has been going about London so when people come to call she'll be able to discuss the sights."

Overton turned pale. "I—ah—I believe they've been too busy getting ready for the come-out to take in many sights."

"Too bad," said the earl nonchalantly. "She will be at a loss for topics of discussion. And if someone mentions the "Folly," which will happen sooner or later since everyone is talking about it, she will appear ignorant." He shrugged. "What a shame. I'm sure you're too busy to bother with a chit. Perhaps she can get a husband just by her looks, though some men do require a little conversation from their wives."

"I'm not too busy," Overton said, pulling at his cravat. "But I don't know where to take her. Or how to make up a party."

The earl frowned. "Well, I did have other plans, but since you're my friend— Well, I suppose I can help you out."

Overton grabbed his hand. "Thank you, you're a true friend. Shall we say tomorrow afternoon?"

"Fine," the earl replied. "I'll be there." He

looked out across the floor. "I say, who is that fellow dancing with Amanda now? He looks old enough to be her father."

Overton sighed. "You're right. I just believe I'll have a word with him." And off he went.

The earl smiled to himself. His plan was working. Tomorrow he'd have Psyche on his arm and—

"You look like the cat that swallowed the cream," Georgie said, appearing at his side and grinning up at him.

"Perhaps I do." He glanced around and lowered his voice. "Tell me, what did she say?"

Georgie frowned. "I tried to pump her, but Psyche's no pea brain. She wouldn't talk."

His impatience was getting the better of him. "What did she say about me?"

Georgie shrugged. "She said you are a man, like any other man."

The world seemed to darken. He was no more to her than any fool that—

"But," Georgie continued, "you must not despair."

"Why not?" he asked eagerly, feeling a surge of hope. "What do you know?"

Georgie grinned. "I know Psyche. She cannot fool me. She likes you."

"But she said—"

Georgie glared at him in exasperation. "Southdon, I think love has addled your wits."

"But—"

"Any sane woman would agree that you're an exceptional man. Since Psyche did not agree, it's very clear."

He groaned. This female approach to things had no logic. "Georgie, please, have mercy on me. What is clear?"

"It's clear she's interested in you."

The breath left his lungs in a great whoosh. "But how do you know—"

"I told you. I know because her disinterest is not reasonable."

And then she smiled brightly and bounced off, leaving him to ponder the peculiarities of the female mind.

Chapter Thirteen

The next afternoon found Amanda, and Psyche, on pins and needles. To Psyche's intense relief, Aunt Anna had gone upstairs for her customary nap still muttering about last night's debacle.

Amanda and Psyche, dressed in their most becoming walking dresses, and with bonnets at the ready, sat in the library, trying to do embroidery. But with little success.

Amanda was too anxious to sit still and Psyche herself was fighting off an attack of nerves. She sighed, picking out another wrong stitch. There was no need to be so anxious. This excursion should go well. And she would have the earl to herself. No Georgie to flirt with him this time.

"Why don't they come?" Amanda demanded for the hundredth time. "Whatever can be keeping them?"

Psyche, who had just been asking herself the same question, though silently, gave Amanda a sympathetic look. "Come away from the window, my dear. You simply must stop twittering about so. Overton has never liked the nervous sort."

"Oh, I am not nervous," Amanda chattered, wringing her handkerchief. "Not really! Not usually. Only last night, when he danced with me, I was even more certain that he is the man I wish to marry. So today is very important."

Poor thing. Psyche could certainly commiserate with her. "Today is only one day," Psyche reminded her. "If my cousin doesn't notice you today, there is always tomorrow."

Amanda frowned, turning back to peer out through the lace panels. "If he doesn't notice me soon, I shall be on the shelf. Permanently on the shelf. Old and wrinkled and—" She turned from the window, her hand to her mouth. "Oh dear, I *am* sorry. You are not old or wrinkled! But I am just such a wreck. Why can't the man see I love him?"

Psyche sighed. "Men are not always the brightest creatures, Amanda my dear. Especially about love. Sometimes we have to help them recognize things that they ought to see for themselves." *As the earl ought to see that I would make him a better wife than Georgie.*

Amanda sighed. "I only wish to be Overton's wife and make him happy." She made a face. "Even if that means having his mama live with us."

Psyche sighed, too, and then smiled. "Never

150

mind that. For a wedding present I will give you lessons on circumventing strange relations like Overton's mama. It can be done. It just takes some practice."

"I shall need—" Amanda began, then at the sound of a carriage she turned to the window again. "He's come!"

Psyche swallowed. The eager welcome on Amanda's face was obviously for Overton. But surely the earl had come, too. He had promised. "Is my cousin alone?"

"No, no. He isn't alone." Amanda turned back. "The earl is with him."

Psyche's heart went back to beating regularly. He had come, just as he'd promised.

"And someone else," Amanda went on. "Your friend, Lady Standish. And the Viscount Gresham."

Psyche's heart sank again. "You mean another carriage has arrived?"

Amanda shook her head. "No, they're all in the earl's landau. Oh, good, Overton is coming to the door!"

Psyche got to her feet. *Why did Georgie have to come?*

Psyche followed Amanda into the foyer just as Overton entered. "There you are," he cried, smiling at Psyche. "I told Southdon you'd be ready. Come, get your bonnets on. We're going to see the Folly."

Amanda, who was already tying her poke bonnet, swung around to ask, "What folly, guardian?"

151

Overton patted her hand and smiled at her. "It's a new scientific museum. Just opened on Piccadilly Street."

Amanda turned her bright blue eyes on the man and smiled sweetly. How incredible, Psyche thought, Overton couldn't see that his ward loved him and it was so completely obvious.

"But why," Amanda inquired, "is it called a folly?"

Overton smiled, a smile so patronizing that Psyche bristled. Whatever was wrong with him? The man needed some common sense.

And what was wrong with her? She was never this waspish. She had to stop thinking about the earl and concentrate on helping Amanda. She had come to London to help the girl, and that was what she meant to do.

"It was just lately established by Lady Elizabeth Farrington, the late Lord Farrington's daughter," Overton explained. "He kept a scientific cabinet—you know, a room for scientific objects—and she decided to enlarge upon it, to open a museum to display his treasures. And some things of her own finding." He grinned cheerfully. "I understand she has quite an outstanding collection of shrunken heads."

Amanda paled, her hands trembling at her bonnet strings. "Real shrunken heads?"

Overton nodded. "Yes, child, but you needn't examine them if they frighten you. I'll admit, it does sound rather grisly."

He ushered them both out the door. "There

152

are other things to see, many other things. But Georgie says the learned pig is the best."

Psyche swallowed another sigh. Georgie again. Was Georgie going to intrude into every situation? And then Overton's words finally registered. "Learned pig?" Psyche could not keep the incredulity out of her voice.

Overton nodded emphatically. "Yes. He counts, you see. Adds and subtracts. Tells the time."

Psyche stopped, halfway down the walk. "Come now, Overton, really. You are bamming us."

"Indeed, he isn't," the earl said, coming up the walk to meet them, a smile lighting his handsome face. "Toby is quite learned. I have seen him perform."

As always, seeing the earl raised Psyche's spirits. He was such a handsome man and today in his coat of claret-colored superfine and fawn inexpressibles, with his Hessians gleaming in the sunlight, he was striking indeed.

And in her blush-colored walking dress and darker rose bonnet, she matched him nicely. What a lovely coincidence.

She gave him a smile, and leaned closer, unable to keep herself from asking, "Why is Georgie here?"

The earl raised an eyebrow. "Oh, I ran into Gresham at the club when I was discussing the thing with your cousin. I thought having him along would be a good idea. And when Georgie

153

heard about our excursion she wished to come, too. I didn't think you would mind."

"Of course not." She minded a great deal, but she couldn't say so, could hardly admit to herself, let alone to him, that she wished Georgie somewhere else. All night Psyche had been thinking about this afternoon, about spending it in the company of the earl. And now Georgie would be coming along. Spoiling things.

Farrington's Museum was housed in a rather nondescript building. Psyche did not remember what it had housed during her Season. When they descended from the landau and the gentlemen offered the ladies their arms, Psyche found herself, somehow, paired with her cousin.

She sent the earl a bewildered look, but he raised one eyebrow a fraction, as though to say she would understand later, and then he turned back to Georgie, who was arrayed in a stunning walking dress of Bishop's blue, exactly the shade of her eyes.

Psyche sighed bitterly. She would never understand why so many men preferred Georgie's company to hers. But deep in her heart she knew it was not "so many men" she was thinking of. Georgie could have all the men in London for all *she* cared. Psyche only wanted the earl.

Gresham had offered Amanda his arm. Now he leaned closer, his reddish hair tousled, his round face alight with mischief, and whispered something to her. For the merest moment her eyes sought Psyche's, then Amanda laughed merrily, as though Gresham were the greatest wit in London.

At Psyche's side, Overton frowned. "I wonder what Gresham said that Amanda finds so funny."

Psyche shrugged. "I wouldn't know." What did it matter, anyway, when Georgie was hanging on the earl's arm and gazing up at him with bright admiring eyes?

But Overton's grumbling brought Psyche's attention back to her ward. Strange, the way Amanda was acting. After all, it wasn't Gresham Amanda wanted to attract. So why was she acting the flirt, ohing and ahing like a green chit?

"Don't like that chap," Overton muttered. "He's too forward by far. Don't know why Southdon had to ask him along."

Gazing at her cousin's disgruntled expression, Psyche suddenly saw. Gresham had been put up to this! He was playing a part, flirting with Amanda to make Overton jealous. She could see it now. That had been the earl's plan all along. And it fit in with Gresham's desire to make Georgie jealous. It seemed to be working, too.

Psyche swallowed a sigh. But none of that accounted for Georgie's behavior; for the merry little laugh that showed her perfect teeth, for the way she clutched the earl's arm as though she couldn't walk alone, for the way she leaned so intimately close to him, resting against his arm. Oh, it was clear, too clear, that Georgie had a plan of her own. A plan to —

"Psyche!" Overton's tone was impatient. "Come on. We're going in."

She let him lead her in after the others. Next time the earl planned an excursion, she was going to stay home. But wouldn't that be even worse torture, wondering what Georgie was doing, what Georgie was saying, what wiles she was exercising on the earl?

And perhaps the earl had had a point in arranging the pairings as he had. If her cousin had been paired with Georgie, he'd have been so busy being charmed by her that he wouldn't have noticed what Amanda was doing at all.

Yes, Psyche conceded, the earl knew what he was doing. But that didn't mean she had to like it. It simply was not fair that Georgie could have any man she pleased. Assuredly she could have the earl; he'd practically said as much.

"Shall we stop to watch the sword swallower?" Gresham inquired of the ladies.

"But of course," trilled Georgie, "that sounds terribly exciting." And she moved even closer to the earl.

Psyche gnawed her bottom lip and kept silent. Coming to London had been a mistake. Lady Bluestocking had not been prepared to find love. She didn't know how to win a man; she only knew how to drive one away.

The little group stopped before a small stage. The sword swallower, one Signor Cavelli, wore red velvet — and being rather round, he much resembled an overripe apple. But the swords and daggers laid out on the black velvet cloth were long and sharp, quite real — and dangerous looking.

"Oh dear," breathed Amanda, clutching Gresham's arm. "How can he swallow such things? The poor man will hurt himself."

"Nonsense," observed Overton, dragging Psyche with him as he moved closer to his ward. "It's not for real. It's some kind of trick." Unfortunately, his voice carried to the stage.

The little Italian stiffened. He drew himself up, throwing looks as sharp as his daggers. "The signor is wrong. Is no tricks here. The Great Cavelli swallows the real daggers." He glared at Overton. "You come up on stage," he offered, waving an expressive hand. "You examine swords. You examine daggers. You see."

Overton frowned and tried to step back out of sight, but Psyche held her ground. If the man was going to issue challenges, he'd better be prepared to face the consequences.

Overton's face slowly turned red. "I meant no harm, Signor Cavelli. Truly." He indicated Amanda. "It's just that I was thinking of the child here. She was frightened. I wanted to calm her fears."

Signor Cavelli pursed his lips. "Surely milord

is joking. This is no child. This is the young lady. *Bellisima* young lady."

Amanda flushed and smiled prettily. "Thank you, sir."

Psyche smiled. The girl did know how to accept a compliment.

Signor Cavelli beamed. "Is no need to thank me. We *paisanos,* we see the beauty, we appreciate the beauty. Such is our way."

The little man made Amanda blush again.

As Overton began grumbling under his breath, Psyche glanced over to see what charms Georgie was presently practicing on the earl and happened to catch his expression. The earl was looking extremely pleased with himself. And why not? Everything was going the way he wanted.

Be sensible, she told herself irritably. *He's getting Overton to notice Amanda.* Psyche sighed. *And Georgie's getting him to notice her.*

But who wouldn't notice Georgie? She was a beautiful, charming woman who knew how to attract men. *She* had no trouble getting a man's attention. Psyche frowned and gnawed on her bottom lip again as Georgie leaned close to the earl once more, smiling up at him with wide, adoring eyes.

Unable to bear it any longer, Psyche turned to Overton. "Cousin, I wish to see the shrunken heads."

He frowned, but after a glance up at the little Italian, who, though he had picked up a sword to swallow, was still beaming down at Amanda, Overton nodded.

"Come," he said to Gresham and Southdon. "Let's move along."

They had turned, moving away from the stage where Signor Cavelli was happily swallowing one, two, three swords at a time, and had gotten halfway across the room when a shrill voice rang out. "Look, Mama, it's Lady Bluestocking!"

Chapter Fourteen

Overton started and then, instead of hurrying them out as any sensible man would have done, he stopped and waited for Miss Linden and her mama to catch up.

The man really was a pea brain, Psyche thought irritably as she prepared to face the obnoxious Lindens. Whatever could Amanda see in him?

The Lindens were panting as they drew near, especially Lady Linden whose ample bosom rose and fell with her breath to quite a startling degree.

"Oh!" Miss Linden gasped, fanning herself with her handkerchief. "We might have missed you in this press of people. What a pity that would have been."

"Yes, indeed," said the earl with an amused look to Psyche. "A terrible pity." He smiled at Miss Linden and that fortunate creature blushed cherry red.

But nothing could keep her from talking. "We

were just saying, Mama and I, that sword swallowing sounds so romantic—dashing and dangerous, you know. But Signor Cavelli is a disappointment. He just doesn't fit the part."

She sighed. "That's to be expected, of course." She lowered her voice to a dramatic whisper. "Everyone is talking about Lady Elizabeth's folly in opening such a place as this. Imagine a woman thinking she can be scientific. How very amusing!"

Psyche swallowed several unladylike words. "I don't find it amusing at all," she said grimly. "I find it quite admirable."

Miss Linden started, sending her a reproachful glance. "But she travels about the country. And Lord Worthington goes with her. She *says* she's looking for objects to display in her museum, but really—"

"I don't see anything wrong with that either," Psyche interrupted. "I'm sure she has someone with her besides Lord Worthington."

Miss Linden shrugged. "Oh, her old nanny and that companion of hers, Sarah somethingor-other. But really, what does that matter? Everyone says—"

"Remember the reading of your cards," Psyche said crisply. "You should not repeat gossip. You don't want to make trouble for yourself."

Miss Linden's thin nose turned pink. "Of course not. I did not mean—"

"Well," interrupted the earl, drawing Georgie

161

toward the other door. "Shall we proceed? I believe the learned pig is in the next room."

Psyche swallowed a curse. What was wrong with the man? The day was going from bad to worse. He might as well have invited the Lindens to take his arm, except that Georgie already had that.

The Lindens exchanged pointed glances. "The learned pig is not that good," Lady Linden pronounced grandly, waving a pudgy beringed hand. "Bullock's has one that's much better. It's smarter. And it does much more."

The earl chuckled. "I'm sorry to disagree, Lady Linden."

He didn't look at all sorry, Psyche thought. He looked quite pleased with himself.

"I think Toby is by far the better pig," the earl continued. "The one at Bullock's doesn't tell time so well. But come along, you'll see for yourself." And to Psyche's disgust, the Lindens did just that.

The pig was big, probably five hundred pounds, and pinkish white but very clean. The man with him was not nearly so big, nor so clean, and he definitely had the look of the country about him.

Could a pig *really* count? Psyche wondered. No, it must be some kind of trick. But animals often were very intelligent. And they could be trained.

Their party moved closer.

"Ladies and gentlemen," the pig's master

cried, standing with his feet planted far apart and looking like he'd just come in from the barnyard. "Let me present Toby. The smartest pig in all of England."

"There's a smarter pig at Bullock's," Miss Linden insisted, elbowing her way to the front of the crowd.

The pig's master looked first amazed, and then hurt. "How can you be saying such a thing? Why, Toby'll be having his feelings hurt!"

The pig gave an agonized squeal and rolled his eyes heavenward, for all the world as if his feelings really *were* wounded.

Psyche swallowed her laughter. Miss Linden had obviously not bargained for a man—or a pig—so well versed in dealing with hecklers.

"Now see what you've gone and done?" the pig's master demanded as Toby sank back on his haunches and lowered his great head between his front legs in an effort to hide it.

"Now, now Toby." The man stroked the pig's huge head. "The lady don't mean nothing by it. She'll apologize, won't you, miss?"

Miss Linden's nose began to quiver and she looked to her mama, but Lady Linden remained silent, obviously unable to come up with a reply.

"You've got to say you're sorry, miss. Else he won't do nothing more. And all those good folks what come to see him'll be mighty disappointed."

The crowd began to mutter, turning to look

at Miss Linden with unfriendly faces.

"You just tell him you're sorry, miss. And he'll go right on. He'll even tell the time for you, he will."

Miss Linden glanced around once more, but finding no help in her mama or anyone else, stammered, "I— I am sorry."

Toby raised his head, shaking it up and down as though to say yes, and gave a squeal that almost sounded like laughter. Then he lumbered to his feet and turned to his master.

Psyche, glancing at the earl, saw his smile and bit back one of her own. Someday, perhaps, Miss Linden would learn not to heckle performers. But somehow Psyche didn't think it would be soon.

"Oh look!" Amanda cried in delight. "He's spelling out his name!"

And indeed he was. With his huge pink snout Toby rooted at the cards that bore the letters in his name. He pushed them around until they spelled TOBY. And when the crowd applauded, the huge pig essayed what looked like a bow.

Amanda turned to her guardian and gave him a fetching smile. "That was the most marvelous thing, guardian. Thank you so much for bringing me today."

Overton looked a trifle surprised, but recovered to say pompously, "You're quite welcome, my dear."

Psyche frowned. It was too bad she couldn't just have a talk with Overton, just point out that Amanda loved him—though in her present waspish mood Psyche could hardly see why—and suggest that he marry his ward himself.

But she couldn't do that. She had given her word of honor to Amanda. And anyway the earl was probably right, Overton was just stubborn enough to disregard her advice. No, they would have to proceed as planned, though "as planned" had certainly not included a meeting with the Lindens.

Miss Linden's altercation with the pig's master seemed to have disabused her of the notion of offering any other challenges to his master. And when Psyche turned, she found to her relief that Miss Linden and her mama had faded into the crowd and vanished.

The earl's party continued, stopping to admire exhibits until they reached the door of a small room. "The shrunken heads are in here," Overton announced. "And I do think they're tastefully displayed."

Psyche frowned. How on earth could the man consider any display of shrunken heads tasteful? But she allowed Overton to lead her to the glass case where four miniature heads, complete with hair and eyes, sat in a row, staring out at the spectators.

"Notice the eyes," Overton observed. "So lifelike. As though they were actually seeing you."

Psyche did not observe anything lifelike about the heads, in fact she thought them rather disgusting, but she had no opportunity to say so.

165

Amanda took one look, raised a hand to her mouth, and gave a little scream.

Then, while Psyche stared in amazement, Amanda swayed once and began to sink slowly toward the floor. In spite of the fact that she had been leaning on Gresham's arm, her swoon took her in the direction of her guardian. With a muttered oath, Overton wrenched free of Psyche and caught Amanda to him before she reached the floor.

And there he stood, looking for all the world like a great booby, clutching Amanda's limp form while her bonnet half covered his face and looked about to poke him in the eye.

"I should have known," he muttered. "The child's too delicate for such sights."

Psyche sighed in exasperation. There he stood, holding what was obviously a woman, and he still persisted in calling her a child. The man was incredible.

"Here," said Georgie, dropping the earl's arm and hurrying over to take charge of the situation. "This way, Overton." She pointed to a bench. "We must lay her flat. Give her some air."

Overton carefully put Amanda down, kneeling beside her with a worried frown.

Psyche was about to step forward, to see if she could be of assistance, when a throaty whisper came from beside her. "Well done." She turned, meeting the earl's dancing eyes. For a moment she thought *she* might swoon. He was

166

so close and she remembered so vividly how wonderful it had felt being carried in his arms.

But unfortunately she had little practice at swooning and the earl had seen so many false swoons he would surely find her out and— Only then did his words register. "You mean—"

The earl nodded. "Georgie suggested it. Gresham thought it would be great fun. Don't worry, they won't blab."

Psyche swallowed her objections. Georgie would be willing to do anything for the earl, certain as she was that he needed a woman of experience, preferably herself. And Gresham— Well, it looked like he wasn't trying to make Georgie jealous, after all, but simply to please her.

Psyche turned to the earl, moving a little nearer. His eyes were full of mischief and suddenly she found herself saying, "So this time the maiden didn't fall into *your* arms."

He chuckled. "No, thank goodness. Catching falling maidens is difficult work, especially since the right ones seldom fall."

She glanced toward Georgie. "Perhaps they're too smart," she said, trying to keep her voice light, though her heart felt quite heavy.

"Perhaps," the earl said, his tone noncommittal.

"Ooooh." Amanda's eyelids fluttered. "What— What happened?"

Overton bent over her, all solicitude. "It was the shrunken heads, my dear. The sight of them

167

Psyche nodded. "Yes, he did. He was one of the few who did." She frowned, remembering those difficult times. "My mama was—" She stopped. Oh dear, what was she thinking? She couldn't tell the earl about Mama. If she did, if he knew all about Lady Bluestocking, knew what a fraud she was, he would no longer see her as safe. He would no longer want to spend time with her.

She swallowed a sigh. Soon, too soon, she would be going back to Sussex. But in the meantime, she wanted every minute she could get with him.

"You were speaking of your mama," the earl said, his dark eyes flashing.

Psyche nodded. She could tell him a little. "Yes. She was much like Aunt Anna except that she kept her figure."

"And your father?"

"He was a quiet man," she said, relieved that the earl did not press her about Mama, "interested in the past. He left dealing with the present up to Mama."

The earl nodded. "His interest accounts for your Greek name."

"Yes. He used to pronounce it the Greek way. He loved all things Greek." She sighed. "I miss him."

Briefly the earl covered her gloved hand with his. "I understand."

Psyche blinked back a sudden rush of tears, but they were not for the loss of Papa but for

170

the impending loss of the earl. Life without the earl's company was going to be so dull, so bleak, so—terribly empty.

"Psyche?"

She turned to find Overton staring at her in frustration.

"Yes, what is it?"

"We simply must find Amanda a husband— and soon. The poor child needs someone to look after her."

Psyche's patience had worn thin. Why couldn't the man see? "She needs—"

"A fine handsome husband," interrupted the earl. "And we will see that she gets one."

"We?" Overton asked, his eyebrows rising.

"Yes," said the earl. "I have agreed to help Psyche with this. You need have no fear. Amanda will be safely wed before the summer is over."

Overton nodded. "That's good." He frowned and pulled at his cravat. "But remember, I must approve the match."

"Of course, of course," the earl soothed. "That is understood."

Overton started back to the others and the earl looked to Psyche. "Well, and what part of London shall we see tomorrow?"

Psyche frowned, trying to think. "The tower perhaps, maybe the menagerie, or Bullock's—"

The earl frowned. "How about the Royal Institution? I am a subscriber there and can get us seats."

"What shall we see there?"

"A demonstration of that discovery called laughing gas, among other things. This Humphrey Davy discovered it not long ago and he uses it to keep patients from suffering pain."

Psyche sent him a peculiar look. "Southdon, I do not really think Amanda is up to seeing anyone in pain."

"Indeed, not," said the earl with a chuckle. "But that was not my intent. Davy lectures on the properties of his gas and then he allows people to inhale it. It produces a certain giddiness and can be very amusing."

She did not see how giddiness could be that amusing, but she really didn't care where they went. As long as she could be with the earl where they were was immaterial.

And then she remembered Georgie. "Will— Will Gresham be going, too?"

The earl nodded. "Of course, I'll ask them now."

And before Psyche could marshal any words, he had dropped her arm and hurried over to the others.

She murmured several oaths that would have shocked her quiet father no end. She had thought she was a woman of some understanding. Papa had always said so and she had believed him. But if she had so much intelligence, then why on earth was she making such a mess of things? Why must she be so inept at love?

Love. The word hung in her mind with dreadful finality. She loved the earl, there was no denying the fact. She was every bit as love struck as young Amanda. And she had even less idea than that young woman how to go about getting the man she loved.

Chapter Fifteen

The earl apparently had no trouble convincing Overton that they should make up a party to go see the laughing gas demonstrated. And so, allowing for one day of rest for Amanda in between their outings, the plans were set.

Psyche took great pains choosing a walking dress of white muslin sprigged with pink flowers. With it she wore a claret-colored Spencer and a chip bonnet tied with a matching claret scarf.

Amanda had chosen a pale blue outfit that brought out the color of her eyes. And, since it sported no ruffles, she looked quite lovely, and seemed most content.

As they entered the Royal Institution, Psyche cast a glance at Overton, beaming down at Amanda like the veriest lovesick calf. How could her cousin be so stupid as not to know that he was in love? A woman now, a woman would know. *She* knew she was in love. She just didn't know what to do about it.

The large room was crowded. It seemed that much of fashionable London had turned out to hear the Davy lecture. The rows of chairs were nearly full and the spectators chattered like magpies, gazing eagerly at the stage where a large work table held several flasks and other apparatus.

The earl led them to seats near the front and saw them all settled before he took a place beside Psyche at the end of the row. Amanda was on her other side, looking up at Overton with glowing eyes.

Her eyes bright with mischief, Amanda turned. "Oh, Psyche," she exclaimed, loud enough for Overton to hear. "They say Professor Davy is quite a fine figure of a man, that he has the most thrilling manner and such magnificent eyes and—"

Overton snorted. "Amanda, really! You shouldn't carry on in such an unseemly fashion."

Amanda winked at Psyche, then opened her eyes wide and turned them on him. "But, guardian, I thought you *wished* me to find a husband. And Professor Davy *is* young, and quite nice to look at, I hear, though I don't know that I care much for the name Humphrey—how should one whisper it tenderly in—"

"Amanda! Really!" Overton's face was now a bright pink and his eyebrows drawn together in a fierce frown.

Still Amanda persisted. "But guard—"

"Enough, I said!" Overton scowled at her. "You're a young woman of breeding. You cannot marry a—a professor! It just isn't done."

Amanda pursed her pink lips into a pout, quite a kissable pout, Psyche noted. How had the girl learned these tricks? To widen her eyes in shocked surprise, to purse her lips so as to invite a man's kisses, to lean enticingly close to a man and so incite—

This was ridiculous! *She* could not do any of those things. She would feel utterly and completely foolish just trying.

She glanced down the row to where Georgie sat in animated conversation with Gresham. Georgie laughed at him, then leaned closer and whacked him on the wrist with her fan.

Psyche sighed. All the world seemed to know how to engage in the ritual of male/female. All the world but Lady Bluestocking! She could not, in her wildest imagination, conceive of behaving as Georgie did—or Amanda, for that matter.

Much as Psyche might love the earl—and she had admitted to herself that she did love him—she could never behave in such a foolish fashion. She sighed again.

The earl leaned closer. "I hope you are not worn out with this work you've undertaken for Amanda," he said with concern.

Psyche straightened. "No, no. I am fine. It's just that sometimes I miss Sussex." And now, she told herself in disgust, she had taken to lying, too. Sussex was actually the farthest thing from her mind.

"I understand," the earl said, his heart falling. If she missed Sussex, she would wish to return there as soon as possible. And if he got Overton to confess too soon to loving Amanda, Psyche would be gone. This called for some delaying tactics. A change in his plans.

He sat back to consider, but while he did so, he let himself feast his eyes on Psyche. She was so beautiful. And so unattainable. Other women would have been flirting with him long ago. But not Psyche. She didn't ever seem to use feminine wiles. Was that because she didn't know how? Or was it because being Lady Bluestocking she saw no need, had no wish for their relations to each other to go any further than this rather tenuous arrangement in behalf of getting Amanda married?

He simply could not tell. And it was driving him crazy. Georgie might insist all she liked that Psyche loved him, *he* still could not believe it. He wanted the words from her own lips, wanted to hear her say "Justin, I love you."

Professor Davy entered the room and the subscribers broke into applause. "Ohhh," cooed Amanda. "He *is* handsome." Then she turned to Overton, put a hand on his sleeve. I'm sorry, guardian, really I am. I'm such a foolish girl. I'm just so fortunate to have you to take care of me."

To Psyche's surprise, this fulsome flattery

made Overton beam. Did love include a man's losing the power of rational thought? she wondered as Overton covered Amanda's gloved hand with his own and actually patted it.

Psyche hid her smile behind a handkerchief.

The earl leaned closer. "Looks quite the fool, doesn't he?"

Psyche nodded, trying to keep her heart from pounding at his closeness. "Yes, but I understand that's part of the affliction. Love makes fools of us all."

The earl raised an eyebrow. "My, my, Lady Bluestocking is a constant surprise to me."

She didn't want to talk about Lady Bluestocking, but she had to ask. "What do you mean?"

He smiled, that brash, mischievous smile she'd come to love.

"I mean that Lady Bluestocking is renowned far and wide for her calloused disregard for love and marriage. Yet you frequently make statements that indicate you find love somewhat less than reprehensible."

"I—" Her heart rose up in her throat. Why hadn't she kept her tongue between her teeth? Now she was in the suds for sure. "I— I—"

He smiled and covered her hand with his own, his touch burning through both their gloves. "In fact, when I had known you but a short while you told me that you had wished to marry for love."

She felt the blood rush to her face, knew her cheeks were turning scarlet. "I— That was long ago, before—before I became Lady Bluestocking."

"Oh, I see," he said, his tone frankly disbelieving.

She tried to pull her hand away, get it free of his, but he would not allow it.

"Have you never considered marriage?" he asked, leaning closer still.

Psyche hesitated, her heart pounding. If she told him yes she had, he would no longer think himself safe with her and she would lose what little time she had left with him. And yet—

"Have you?" he persisted, his hand still holding hers.

She swallowed a sigh. "Of course not," she replied, keeping her voice bright and teasing. "Don't you remember? A woman needs a husband like a fish needs wings."

The strangest expression crossed his face. It could not be disappointment, perhaps it was distaste, because she had repeated her unwomanly sentiment yet one more time.

Then his face cleared and he chuckled, patting her hand again. "Of course. I had rather forgotten. Too bad."

Too bad about what? Psyche wanted to know, finally able to withdraw her fingers. But while she was trying to muster the courage to ask, Professor Davy called the audience to order and began his lecture.

Nitrous oxide, as laughing gas was rightly called, appeared to be a most interesting chemical. But Psyche found the professor's lecture difficult to follow. She had no need to inhale any gas to induce giddiness—the earl's presence was more than sufficient to make her lightheaded—and the professor, though his style of delivery was lively, seemed to suffer from a kind of awkwardness with words which made his thoughts somewhat abstruse. Added to that was her own inability to keep her mind off the earl.

Finally she gave up and let her thoughts slip where they would. She recalled every minute she had spent with the earl, second by second, savoring her memories. They would have to last a lifetime, those memories, since if before she had not married because she did not love, now she would not marry because she *did* love. She loved the best catch in London, a man determined not to be caught, a man who sought her company only because it was safe.

She sighed and stirred restlessly in her chair, turning so she could see Amanda. The girl was gazing at the stage with rapt attention. And beyond her Overton sat scowling fiercely.

The earl leaned closer, letting his eyes feast on Psyche. If only there were some way to tell what she was thinking. "A useful emotion, jealousy," he ventured. "Amanda plays it well."

Psyche merely nodded, her face grave.

"Do *you* think jealousy a useful emotion?" he asked.

She frowned, obviously puzzled. "Useful in what way?"

He smiled. "In bringing people together." He was treading on dangerous ground here and he knew it, but he wanted to hear her thoughts on the matter, to discover what she believed. Or just to hear the sound of her sweet voice.

She nodded. "I've heard of such things but —"

Professor Davy looked out over the crowd. "Ladies and gentlemen, I need a volunteer. Some good soul who will be willing to demonstrate how this amazing gas dulls the senses and obviates pain."

The professor waited, but there was no response from the audience. "Come now," he called. "It's not dangerous. Not at all."

People looked at each other, twittering nervously, but still no one replied. The earl leaned toward Psyche. "I dare you," he whispered, mischief in his eyes.

"Oh no." Psyche frowned. She didn't intend to be made a fool of, to perform some ridiculous thing while people watched, and laughed at her. She smiled at him with artificial sweetness. "Why don't you go?"

He shook his head. "I have already experienced the effects of the gas." He frowned and stroked his chin. "So, it appears I am to be disappointed today. I thought Lady Bluestocking was game for anything."

He was doing it again! Throwing Lady Bluestocking up to her! Daring her! But she wouldn't take this bait. She couldn't.

And then Amanda spoke. "Oh, guardian," she cried. "How disappointing! No one is volunteering. I know! I shall do it myself."

Overton practically growled. "You'll do no such thing."

Amanda pouted prettily. "But, guardian, I want to see—"

"I will do it," Overton said, rising to his feet and starting forward.

Psyche turned quickly to the earl. "I never thought—"

"Nor I," he returned, a bemused expression creeping over his face.

Overton reached the front of the room. He looked rather stiff, Psyche thought, and more than a trifle anxious, but he straightened his shoulders.

"Ah," cried Professor Davy. "We have a volunteer. Come forward, brave soul, and let us see you."

Overton stepped forward, smiling nervously. "What must I do?"

"You simply lean over here," Professor Davy indicated. "And breathe deeply."

Overton sent Amanda a look that said "I'm doing this for you" and then he bent over the retort.

A few moments later he was laughing and cavorting around the work bench like a man possessed.

Psyche frowned. "He's going to be up in the

boughs when he finds out what a fool he's made—" But the earl was already on his feet.

He reached the front of the room just as Overton took another big whiff of the gas and began to sway dizzily. "Come on, old fellow," the earl said firmly. "Come back to your seat."

Overton smiled crookedly. *My word,* Psyche thought, *the man behaves as though he's foxed.* Laughing gas appeared to be quite a powerful intoxicant.

The earl led Overton back to his seat, one arm firmly around his shoulders, and pressed him down. "Sit still now," he ordered. "Till the effects of the gas wear off."

Overton scowled and started to get up, but Amanda put a determined hand on his arm. "Really, guardian she said, her voice sweet yet steady. "You must rest for a minute."

"Don't call me guard—guardian," Overton mumbled. "Call—call me Phil—Phillip."

Amanda blinked, obviously surprised by such a request. Then she gazed up at him with adoring eyes. "Yes, Phillip. You are so brave, so strong."

"Nothing," he said. "Nothing to it. Just breathe."

"Still," Amanda insisted. "It was very brave."

Amanda's eyes glowed with love. Psyche swallowed a sigh. Couldn't that fool Overton *see?*

Georgie leaned forward from her place on Overton's other side. "Really, Overton, it was rather brave. *Some* men would never consider

183

doing such a thing." She sent Gresham a sharp look. "Some men don't care about the women they're with."

Gresham flushed, obviously hurt. Why didn't Georgie have more care for the man's feelings?

"It's all a silly business," Psyche intervened. "And may even be dangerous. Professor Davy may know a great deal about this gas, but he cannot know everything."

Georgie shrugged. "If it were dangerous, the Institution wouldn't allow these demonstrations."

Psyche had no answer for that and, though she did change her position to smile at Gresham, the man looked distinctly uncomfortable. Georgie was being most unfair to him. If the earl had ever felt about her as Gresham did about Georgie, Psyche thought, she would never—

Smiling, she turned to Georgie. "Why don't you go? Surely a woman is just as capable as a man of breathing."

Beside her, the earl made a startled noise, but she ignored him and continued to watch Georgie.

Georgie hesitated for a few minutes, then she got to her feet and looked at Gresham. "Psyche is right. I will not ask you to do anything I wouldn't do."

Though Gresham looked a little green around the gills, he jumped to his feet, too. "I won't allow you to do it alone."

Georgie grinned. "Then we'll do it together.

We'll be part of a scientific experiment."

"About as scientific as the learned pig!" Psyche muttered.

But Amanda was concerned with Overton, who was still giggling inanely, and Georgie and Gresham were on their way to the work bench where Professor Davy beamed a welcome. Only the earl responded, probably only he had heard.

"I believe," he whispered, "that the learned pig is somewhat more entertaining."

Psyche smiled. "He was amusing."

The earl stored this information, along with wonder at the beauty of her smile. He would have to see that they visited Farrington's Folly again. Anywhere that Psyche wanted to go, he would take her. Strange, he thought, how she had invaded his life, taken it over to a degree that he had allowed no other woman, never thought of allowing another woman. And yet he liked it.

He glanced at Overton, still grinning like a silly ass. The man didn't know it yet, but he'd given himself away with that request that Amanda use his name. Amanda would do it, all right, and hearing his Christian name on the lips of the woman he loved would sink him deeper in the mire.

The earl smiled and shifted his weight, bringing him a few inches closer to Psyche. He was not a man to give up. Someday Psyche would be his. He sighed. But this waiting was getting on his nerves.

Of course, Georgie should know more about a woman's feelings than he did. The workings of the female mind had always been a mystery to him, though previously he'd had no trouble getting what he wanted. He had no doubt practically any woman in the ton would find him a suitable husband. But Psyche was not any woman, she was Lady Bluestocking.

Psyche leaned forward. Gresham and Georgie had reached the stage. Gallantly, Gresham went first. His face had turned so pale that even at a distance his freckles were visible. He ran a hand through his hair, looking like an awkward schoolboy.

"Just lean over," the professor encouraged. "Take a deep breath."

Gresham gave Georgie a strange look and then he inhaled. He straightened, smiling idiotically. "Nothing to it," he cried, bending again. He took several more breaths. "Nothing at all."

He straightened again and waved a hand grandly at Georgie. Then his eyes rolled up in his head and while they watched in shock the man slowly sank to the floor.

"Gresham!" Georgie screamed, rushing to break his fall.

The earl was instantly on his feet, hurrying forward to help.

"It's nothing to worry about." Professor Davy soothed the murmuring crowd. "The gentleman just inhaled too much, too rapidly. He will recover as soon as he breathes in some regular air."

When the earl had helped her lay Gresham flat, Georgie got to her feet. "This is terrible," she cried, rounding on the startled professor. "You should not be allowed to do such—"

"Georgie!" The earl saw that he must take things in hand immediately or he would have a hysterical female on his hands. He grabbed her by the arms and pulled her off to one side. "Easy now, Georgie. Gresham will be all right. I've seen it happen before." He shook her lightly. "And besides there's no need for you to act the fishwife. Why, the way you're carrying on a man would think—"

She started up at him, tears in her incredible blue eyes, and then it came to him. How could he not have noticed it before? "Good Lord, Georgie! You and Gresham?"

"Quiet!" She looked around, then glared at him. "No one must know. You'll spoil our plans for you and Psyche."

"But, Georgie, the man's head over heels and you don't give him any hope."

"He has hope," Georgie said, a little smile creeping over her face. "And when we have you and Psyche safely wed, I may listen to him with more willingness."

Her smile broadened. "This was a brave thing he did today. He was frightened but he did it for me. I admire him for it." She frowned at the earl. "But you needn't tell him so, understand?"

"Of course I understand. You and Gresham! Well, I'll be!" He sighed. "Tell me, Georgie. How much longer is it going to take? When will Psyche be mine?"

Georgie sighed, too. "I can't tell. You know love can't be rushed."

Oh yes, he knew that very well. And he knew something else: The minute Overton discovered his love for Amanda, he himself meant to propose to Psyche. And if he had to follow her back to Sussex and camp on her doorstep like a Gypsy till she said yes, well, he would do that, too.

Chapter Sixteen

In the days that followed the earl saw to it that the six of them frequented most of the sights of fashionable London: the tower, the menagerie, Bullock's, the exhibition of art at the Royal Academy. He arranged excursions to every conceivable attraction within driving distance and almost always, except when Georgie insisted on doing the jealousy thing, he paired himself with Psyche.

She told him that male callers flocked to the house on Grosvenor Square, but Amanda spurned each and every one. And those who still persisted, Overton turned off with harsh words. But the man still made no move himself.

And so one August afternoon, having exhausted all of London's attractions, the earl scheduled a return to Farrington's Folly. Helping Psyche descend from the carriage, he found himself wishing, as he had so often lately, that Overton would stop being such a pompous ass and recognize what was so obviously before his eyes. But the man simply refused to see. And Amanda, no matter what anyone said to her, adamantly refused to even consider another man.

The earl swallowed a sigh. And then there was Psyche! Psyche was always pleasant, not cruel to him as Georgie was on occasion to Gresham. And sometimes the earl was sure—or almost sure—that what he saw in Psyche's eyes was much more than friendship. But still he hesitated.

Perhaps he only *thought* he saw, perhaps it was wishful thinking on his part, perhaps to Psyche he was only a friend. And if that were true, a proposal of marriage would surely make her see him as no friend at all—and she would drive him from her side in anger and frustration.

He tucked her arm in his—at least she allowed him that—and followed the others into the museum.

Amanda, hanging on Overton's arm, was looking up at him in that sickening way of young females in love. The earl stifled another sigh. The chit looked ridiculous, all wide-eyed and glowing like that. And yet—he would give a great deal to have Psyche gaze at him in that very same way.

He glanced down at her, but as usual she was looking around. No wide-eyed awe from Lady Bluestocking. In fact, sometimes she scarcely spoke to him at all.

He glanced at the exhibit before which they

had halted, a rather sorry arrangement of primitive weapons presided over by a harshly painted wooden figure. From the looks of its feathered headdress, this display was supposed to portray savages from the Americas.

"Fierce-looking devil, isn't he?" he inquired, bending to Psyche.

She smiled. "Yes. And I suppose even fiercer if one met him when she was alone and defenseless."

His heart rose up in his throat at the picture — Psyche, his beautiful Psyche, at the mercy of some heathen savage. He swallowed. Thank God such a thing couldn't happen here. This was a civilized —

A shriek echoed from the interior of the museum. It was followed by another — and then a whole series of screams and shrieks, cries and yells. Pandemonium broke loose and people came rushing out, streaming down the corridor, shoving and trampling all before them.

The earl did not stop to think, but immediately swung Psyche behind him, backing her into a corner against the wall, imposing his own body between her and the panicked crowd. Whatever was out there causing such terror, it would reach Psyche only over his dead body. He braced himself and waited.

Behind him, Psyche stood silent, her heart pounding, her cheek pressed against his back. Everything had happened so fast — the screams, the pandemonium, the rioting crowd. She supposed she ought to be frightened — something was certainly very wrong here.

And yet the pounding of her heart, the trembling of her limbs—those were not due to fear at all, but to the inescapable fact that the earl's body was pressing her into the wall, into safety. Except, of course, that what she felt for him left her far from safe.

She waited, every sense alert, every nerve recording the feel of his broad back, his strong shoulders against her. And then, inexplicably, the earl began to laugh, deep hearty laughter. He didn't sound hysterical—and of course he was not a man to be frightened. But this was not a matter for laughter either.

She tried to peer around him, but his shoulders were so broad there wasn't enough room, she could see nothing. She tugged at his sleeve. "Southdon! Tell me! Please. What is so funny?"

He stepped aside, so suddenly that she almost fell and he had to put out a hand to catch her by the elbow.

She caught her breath and then she saw. "Why, it's Toby, the learned pig."

"Yes," said the earl.

"But why—"

"Apparently he was running loose and he frightened someone, thus causing the riot."

She drew herself erect, straightening her bonnet, painfully conscious that the earl was no longer as close to her as she would like. "I—Thank you. You—you risked your life for me."

She gazed up at him, but he said nothing. If only this rescue meant something, something special to him. But it didn't. He had rescued her before. Should the occasion arise he would rescue her again. He was that sort of a man.

But standing there in the deserted exhibit room, hanging onto his arm, Psyche faced the truth. She had made a real mess of things by coming to London. Every day that passed made her love the earl more, made her see how impossible that love was. And every day that passed made her feel the pain more deeply.

She had to get Amanda married. And then Lady Bluestocking had to return to the country. Given time—years perhaps—she might be able to forget the earl. Though she doubted it.

His dark face was full of concern. "Are you all right? I didn't hurt you, did I?"

She almost laughed at the irony of it. "No," she murmured. "I am fine. But what happened?"

His frown smoothed out. "Evidently the pig ran amok. Five hundred pounds of porker coming at one could be rather frightening."

Psyche sighed. "Yes, but—" She pointed toward the pig, now squatting complacently on his haunches and examining his front feet. "How can anyone be afraid of Toby?"

The earl shrugged. "In a crowd panic is easily aroused."

"Toby! Toby, now you come on." The pig's master appeared, a little unsteady on his feet. "Toby, you come on now. We'll get us a nice bucket." He lowered his voice, apparently unaware that they could still hear him. "A nice bucket of gin."

With a little squeal the pig lumbered to his feet and started off toward the back of the museum. The earl turned back to Psyche. "Well, it appears the pig imbibes." He smiled. "Now, where can our friends have gotten to?"

Psyche flushed. She had quite forgotten Amanda and the others. "Perhaps in all the confusion they went outside."

"Perhaps." He stared down at her for the longest moment. Her heart pounded faster, faster, harder, harder. Slowly he bent his head, his face came closer, closer, and—

"There you are!"

The earl straightened, biting back a curse. Trust Overton to arrive at just the wrong moment. Why couldn't— He pulled himself up short. It was probably just as well. If he kissed Psyche, as he had been so tempted to do, kissed her in a public place yet, she would have been horrified. Perhaps she would even have shunned his company ever after.

"We were just coming to look for you," he said. Psyche's hand still lay on his arm. He felt it tremble, but he dared not look at her. Had she read his intent in his eyes? Did she know what he had almost done? "Where are the others?" he asked.

Overton frowned. "I left Amanda outside, with Gresham and Georgie." He pulled at his cravat. "The poor child was absolutely terrified."

The earl swallowed a sigh and asked, "Shall we go get them?"

Overton scowled and seemed in danger of completely ruining his cravat. "I don't want to bring Amanda back in here now. She has such a fragile constitution."

The earl almost snorted. Fragile, indeed! The chit was strong as a horse and a deuced poor actress besides. That kind of fragility had passed with the previous century.

The women he knew used other wiles—the fluttering eyelash, the flattering word, the unexpected press of a bosom against a man's arm. They gazed adoringly into his eyes and fell weakly into his arms. And it was all the sheerest fakery. Not one of them had experienced a genuine emotion. Not one of them had really loved him. And not one of them was worth Psyche's little finger.

"Amanda will be disappointed," Psyche pointed out. "If you don't want to bring her back in here, let us at least go somewhere else."

"Capital idea," said the earl. "How about a ride to Rotten Row?"

Overton hesitated and Psyche persisted. "The change of scenery will be good for Amanda."

"Well—" Overton sighed. "I suppose we could do that."

When they reached Hyde Park and descended from the earl's landau, Gresham offered Georgie his arm, Overton gave his to Amanda, and Psyche found herself bringing up the rear with the earl, a situation certainly to her liking.

"Southdon," she said when the others were

195

out of earshot. "We must do something. We must make Overton see the truth."

The earl frowned. "But how? Our best tactic seems to be patience."

"Pa—" Psyche paused and lowered her voice. "Patience, indeed! We could wait till hel—"

He frowned, his lips thinning into a disapproving line.

"Till next year or the year after," she continued, changing her remark somewhat out of deference to his look. "Waiting simply will not work. We must do something. And we must do it now."

The earl frowned. If only she knew how impatient he was to have this thing settled. "What do you suggest?"

"I don't know, but we must do something." She frowned, her lovely forehead wrinkling in concentration.

"Things certainly used to be much simpler," he observed. "A man just swooped down, like a bird of prey, and took his woman away." He hoped to raise her ire, to divert her from Amanda and her problem to a diatribe on men and their ridiculous customs.

But Psyche was not so easily distracted. She wrinkled her nose in distaste and said, "There's got to be a way, some way to— That's it!"

She stopped so suddenly, clutching his arm in a death grip, that he almost lost his balance and pulled them both down.

"I say," he protested. "You'll have us both on the ground in a minute. And Overton won't like that the least bit."

"But I've got it!" Psyche cried.

She was lovely in her excitement — eyes sparkling, cheeks rosy, bosom heaving. But he did wish she'd make more sense. "What have you got?" he inquired politely, shifting his gaze to her face.

She grinned. "I've got a way to make Overton recognize his love for Amanda."

"You have?"

"Yes. We'll have Amanda abducted."

"Abducted?" Had the woman lost her mind? "Psyche, be sensible. Amanda may not be as fragile as Overton believes, but I really don't think she could handle abduc —"

"No, no," Psyche interrupted in obvious irritation. "Not a real abduction, a fake one."

"A fake one," he repeated, wondering if the woman he loved had lost her mind.

"Yes, it will work superbly. We'll have her abducted. When Overton finds out, he'll be absolutely frantic." She smiled happily. "And at last he'll recognize that he loves her."

"Psyche." This really was a bubble-brained scheme. Even a man in love could see that. "Really, the girl's reputation —"

"It will be safe enough," she insisted stubbornly. "That's the beauty of the whole thing. I shall be with her all the time. Surely no one can doubt Lady Bluestocking."

He hesitated. She had something there. "But if the girl's to be abducted someone must do it."

She nodded vigorously. "Of course. You."

"Me! Of all the harebrained—"

She stiffened and pulled her arm from his. "Might I remind you, milord, that your way has not been at all successful? And you have had the entire summer, too."

She was right about that. He couldn't deny it. Still—"I cannot be the abductor," he began.

"Well, if you won't help—"

He swallowed a curse. How could he love such an obstinate woman? "I didn't say I wouldn't help, but I can't be the abductor."

She stopped and put her hands on her hips, lovely hips he noticed. "And why not?"

"Because Overton will not believe it of me. Think, Psyche. I am Overton's friend. If I want Amanda, I have only to ask. So why on earth should I run off with her?"

He was right. Psyche sighed. Was there no end to this torture? She had to get Amanda and Overton married, get herself away from this pain. "Well then, we'll have to think of someone else. Now who?"

"Psyche, really—"

Why must he frown like that, as though she'd suddenly taken leave of her senses? She was an intelligent woman. And this was an ideal plan. She put a hand on his sleeve. "Surely you must see—this plan will work."

"It will throw Overton into a perfect frenzy," the earl said. "Surely you don't wish that."

Psyche frowned. Why must the man be so dense? "Of course I do. When he discovers that

she is gone, he will realize that he loves her
And he will act accordingly."

"Will he?" the earl inquired. "How can you
be so sure?"

Psyche swallowed a sigh. "I can't, of course.
But we must try. Amanda is getting fr_____
talking of wasting away, declining into the ___
and the like."

"Good Lord! Where did she get an idea ___
that?"

Psyche frowned. "I'm not sure, from s_
thing she's been reading, I suppose."

"What sort of drivel has the chit been ___
now?"

"Well, she mentioned a Mister Richard___
and a heroine of his named—let me thi__
Clarissa."

"Oh no!" cried the earl.

Psyche turned to him. "What is it? W__
wrong?"

"Did she tell you anything about
Clarissa?"

Psyche shrugged. "Only that she admired __
greatly."

His face darkened. "Damnation!"

"Southdon! You're frightening me."

The earl put a reassuring hand over hers__
don't mean to do that, but, Psyche,
Clarissa dies."

"Dies!" Psyche stopped right in the path,
livious to the people passing on either si__
"Not from—"

"Yes," the earl went on. "She wastes a__

199

Psyche did her best
loan of Mr. Richards_
from Amanda, pleadin_
about it that she simpl_

Amanda pressed the
gerly and Psyche com___
was even worse than t_
Richardson's Clarissa _
Defiled by a man wh_
chose death over dish___
death—wasting away, _

Finishing the leng__
Psyche cursed and fl___
floor. This was the m__
in a long time. "She _
muttered, pacing bac_
carpet. "Killed him a__
drel. And I should lik__
son a thing or two! __
a woman with some___
male heads with such__

She paced for some minutes longer, until she was able to control herself. She had to be calm to decide how to approach Amanda. Unfortunately, Amanda was too much like Overton when it came to taking advice. Give advice directly and it was sure to be ignored. Inject it subtly and it might be heeded. And that, thought Psyche, was how she would prepare her strategy.

Next morning Psyche sallied forth to breakfast ready to do battle—though indirectly—with the perfidious Mr. Richardson.

Amanda was already at the table, attacking—what was for the fragile creature she purported to be—an immense plate of food. She looked up eagerly. "Have you finished it? Wasn't it marvelous?"

Psyche sighed deeply. "Oh yes. I do admire Clarissa."

Amanda nodded. "I knew you would."

Psyche poured herself a cup of tea, chose a single tiny biscuit, and sank wearily into a chair. "Yes," she said heavily. "Clarissa is quite right. Life is hardly worth the effort."

Amanda looked up, her bright eyes widening in amazement, a sausage suspended halfway to her mouth.

"Yes," Psyche continued. "I really believe Clarissa is correct. It's far better to pass over to the other side." She sighed again and tried to look melancholy, not too difficult a task considering her unrequited feelings for the earl.

202

Amanda eyed the plate Psyche had in front of her, frowning at its emptiness. "Psyche, you must eat more than that!"

Psyche stared down at the minuscule biscuit. "I've no appetite," she said feebly. "I believe I shall just go back to bed."

"But Psyche—"

"The Lindens are right," Psyche continued in dejected tones. "I have no husband and my life is ruined. I might as well give up."

Amanda put down her fork and shoved her plate aside. "Psyche, this is ridiculous." She looked so serious Psyche almost broke into laughter. "You can't mean to tell me that you intend to waste away. Why— Why, I can't believe it."

Psyche sipped her tea, keeping her gaze carefully lowered. "You mean wasting away is not an appropriate action for a woman?"

"Of course it isn't. That's all silliness and— Oh!" Amanda laughed a little shakily and clapped a hand to her mouth. "I see! Psyche, you devil you, you've been bamming me!"

Psyche looked up, allowing herself a small smile. "Not really. I just wanted you to see. You're a sensible girl, Amanda, you know that. And I'm sure we'll succeed in this. Overton will come around."

Amanda nodded, but she looked about to burst into tears. "I really feel he loves me, but he won't speak, he won't offer for me. Whatever is wrong with the man?"

Psyche sighed. "Who's to know? But listen, I have this plan."

* * *

By the first week in September everything was in place. Planning and plotting, the earl and Psyche had tried to consider every contingency. Psyche felt that they were close to success. She hoped they were close to success. They had to succeed, she told herself firmly. Amanda, at least, had to be happy.

The afternoon before the abduction was scheduled, Psyche and the earl walked alone in the garden, reviewing the final details. "Gresham will provide the carriage," the earl said.

Psyche nodded. "And Georgie will inform Overton."

The earl frowned. "I cannot do it because he would expect me to have set out immediately on hearing such news." He stroked his chin. "But it must be perfectly timed. I must be there so I can offer to go with him." His frown deepened. "Overton can be overblown, you know. Once his ire is up, he may attack someone."

His mind was on her plan, but a little corner of it was experiencing concern. There was something different about Psyche today — a resigned quality he had never sensed in her before. He wasn't sure what such a quality might portend, but resignation did not fit well with Psyche, his brave, resilient Psyche. This feeling made him definitely uneasy.

She turned to him, her lovely face wrinkling into a frown. "He would not actually hurt

Gresham, would he?"

"I don't think so," the earl replied. "And if all goes well, he will not even suspect what we've done. But I must be there to be certain."

Psyche nodded. "And I must be with Amanda and Gresham. To protect her good name."

"Correct. So that leaves Georgie to deliver the message. No doubt she'll manage to come along with us." He searched Psyche's face, watching for something, some little nuance of feeling that might give her away, but he saw nothing.

"No doubt," Psyche repeated, her face expressionless.

Then and there he made up his mind. When this pseudo-abduction was concluded, whatever its outcome, he meant to propose to Psyche. And he did not intend to take no for an answer. Some way he would convince her that marriage to him was right and proper, that Lady Bluestocking should be laid to rest—at long last.

"Georgie can do it," he said. "She's very good at such things."

"You mean she's good at deception," Psyche said evenly.

He gave her a sharp look. A slight flush had darkened her cheeks and her lower lip trembled ever so slightly.

"Yes," he agreed. "Georgie is much better at that kind of thing than you."

To his surprise Psyche blushed even more. "I meant that as a compliment," he explained, feeling as inept as a witless schoolboy.

Psyche nodded, but did not meet his gaze. "I

accept it as one. Thank you."

"So," the earl went on. "Here's what you must tell Amanda to do."

The next day Psyche thought the time for the abduction would never arrive. Through the long afternoon that preceded it, she alternated between being quite sure they would succeed and being quite sure they would fail. But whatever her convictions, her whole consciousness was laced with sadness.

Whatever the outcome of their plan, Overton would soon know the truth. And relieved of her responsibility for Amanda's marriage, Psyche could return to Sussex.

It was not a happy prospect. Once she had loved her estate. But then once she had vowed never to return to London again. That had been her mistake, coming to London. That was one thing she was sure of. And now when she went back to the land she loved she would only be part of a person. Her heart, her stubborn, stubborn heart, would remain in London, would remain with the man who thought of her only as a friend.

Finally Amanda came downstairs wearing a fetching walking dress of Bishop's blue and a matching bonnet. She turned. "Do I look all right?"

"Yes, indeed," Psyche said. "You look most fetching. But do remember to look frightened when Overton arrives at the inn."

Amanda nodded. "Oh, I shall. I want him to be terrified for me." She frowned, clutching her reticule with trembling fingers. "Oh, Psyche, if this doesn't work, whatever shall we do?"

Psyche frowned. "I'm not sure. But our plan *will* work. It has to work. Come, the carriage is waiting."

As usual, White's was crowded with gentlemen. The earl glanced at his watch then back across the table at Overton. He wasn't sure White's was the best place for Georgie to find them but it had seemed the most natural.

The club was too public for his taste. If Georgie got carried away with her performance and forgot the necessity for secrecy — Or if when he heard the news, Overton ran amok — Word would travel all over London faster than the speed of the Lindens' chattering tongues, and Amanda's reputation would be ruined, really ruined.

It was for that reason that he had at first opposed Psyche's plan. It still looked chancy, but it was too late to draw back now. He watched the dealer pass out the cards, picked up his hand, and considered his—

"Overton!" Georgie's entrance was nothing if not dramatic. Her face was so white he wondered if she'd powdered it and her hands fluttered wildly. The club's majordomo, his face wrinkled in agitation, hovered behind her.

"What is it?" Overton asked impatiently. "Don't you know women can't come in here?"

"I must speak to you." She glanced around fearfully. "It will have to be in private."

Overton sighed. "Georgie, I just got my hand. I can't leave now."

Georgie tugged at his sleeve. "You must! Please!" She glanced at the earl. "You, too. We will need you."

Overton looked startled, as though finally realizing her urgency. He glanced at the cards, then back at Georgie who was staring at him with big appealing eyes.

She was doing a bang-up job, the earl thought. If he hadn't been in on the thing, he'd have been really thoroughly alarmed.

Overton pushed back his chair and got to his feet. "I'll be back shortly," he said to the others.

"Me, too," the earl said.

Conscious that all eyes were upon them, he followed Georgie and Overton outside.

"Now," Overton said in that pompous tone. "What is it, Georgie? What's so important?"

Georgie looked suitably upset, wringing her hands. "Amanda. It's Amanda."

"Amanda!" Overton's face went white. Now she had the man's attention. "What about Amanda?"

"She—"

The earl tensed—this was the critical moment.

"She's been abducted!"

Overton looked thunderstruck, his face slowly paling. Finally he shook his head. "It can't be. Come now, Georgie, this is a joke."

Georgie looked to the earl and he saw that she was close to giving way. In a minute she'd be laughing outright. "No," he said hastily. "I think we'd better listen. Georgie, do you know who—"

"No, I didn't recognize the man, but I sent Gresham to follow them. And I came looking for you."

Overton straightened his shoulders, his face setting in lines of grim determination. "We must find her. The poor child will be terrified."

Georgie gave him a look of complete exasperation. "Oh, Overton, you're such a fool!"

The man stared at her, amazed. "A fool? Me?"

"Amanda is not a child," Georgie went on. "She's a young woman—*woman*—and it's past time you recognized that!"

Overton looked about to get into an argument with Georgie, of all things. The earl intervened. "How was Gresham to let us know where they went?"

Overton's face cleared. "Yes! We can't stand around like this. We have to find her."

"We were in his carriage," Georgie said. "I jumped out to come to you and he followed them. He said he'd send a groom to the house."

Overton nodded. "Then we must go home immediately." He turned toward the door of the club.

"Wait!" The earl grabbed him by the sleeve. "Remember, you must not let on to the others. Amanda's reputation—"

"I understand. Come, we must hurry."

Back at the table, Overton laughed. It was a trifle hollow, but considering the circumstances the earl found it sufficient. "Sorry," Overton said to the other players. "We've got to go. The women need us." He chuckled. "You know how it is. Some little hubbub they can't handle on their own."

Psyche would have been incensed by such a statement, the earl thought, following the others to the carriage. She would say that women were very good at handling things on their own. And she might be right about that. But she was wrong about this husband thing. And he wasn't at all sure about this abduction.

When they reached the house, Gresham's groom was waiting. "They're headed toward Gretna Green all right. Milord Gresham is still following 'em. He said to tell you they'll probly get as far as the Boar's Head on the road north."

Overton nodded. "Good job, man." He turned to Georgie. "You can wait here."

Georgie frowned. "But—"

"It's not going to be a pretty sight," Overton said. "When I catch the scoundrel—"

"Amanda will be upset," Georgie pointed out. "She'll need a woman."

Swallowing a smile, the earl settled back. It was apparent no one was going to cheat Georgie out of a firsthand seat at this spectacle. "We're wasting time," he said. "Hadn't we better get going?"

Overton sent one long, exasperated look in Georgie's direction, then apparently resigned himself to her presence. "All right. But you'll have to keep out of the way." He called up to the driver, "The road to Gretna Green. And hurry!"

Then he leaned back, frowning. "I wonder which of those bounders it was. I've turned off so many."

"We'll find out soon enough," the earl said calmly. "Of course, none of this would have happened if the chit had been safely married."

Overton frowned fiercely. "She didn't want any of those suitors. Fribbles, she called them. Told me to send them all away."

"Well," the earl remarked casually. "If you're not careful, you'll end up having to marry her yourself."

"Myself!" Obviously the idea had not crossed the besotted man's mind.

"Yes. You're a man of property. You can—"

From her corner of the carriage, Georgie tittered. "Really, Southdon, Amanda wants a younger—"

"I am not old," Overton interjected with a scowl.

"Indeed not," agreed the earl. "And Amanda does tend to be a little flighty. She needs an older man, a firm hand."

Georgie tittered again. "It's a good thing Psyche didn't hear you say that."

Overton scowled even more. "It's quite true. The girl's a trifle scatterbrained. Not that it detracts from her charm."

"And she's used to you," the earl went on. He examined his cuff. "But marriage—that would mean giving up your freedom. And of course she might prefer someone else."

"She hasn't yet," Overton said, ignoring the remark about losing his freedom. He took a deep breath. "I'll do it!" he cried. "I'll kill the cowardly scum that took her and then I'll ask her to be my wife!"

In her corner, Georgie heaved a huge sigh. The earl knew exactly how she felt. It had been touch and go for a while there, but now if Overton didn't suspect anything when they found Amanda, they should be able to bring it off. Love would triumph. Amanda and Overton would be happy. Gresham and Georgie would be happy.

He swallowed a sigh. And then there was Psyche. He could wait no longer to ask her. With Amanda safely married, Psyche would be intent on going back to Sussex. He had to propose even though he was still no surer of an affirmative answer.

A fine pickle for a man of his stripe, he thought ironically, a man any woman in London would jump at the chance to marry—or so Georgie insisted. And here he was, as nervous as any green schoolboy trying to win a smile from the object of his affections.

Chapter Eighteen

In due course the carriage arrived at the Boar's Head. But by that time all its occupants were on edge.

When the carriage halted, Overton leaped out, glaring madly around. "Where is he? I'll kill him!"

"Easy, man," the earl cautioned. This whole thing was making him more and more uneasy. He loved Psyche but some of her ideas were less than brilliant. And this one in particular . . . "We'll find her." He turned to help Georgie down. "Gresham should be around here somewhere."

When Overton stomped off toward the inn, Georgie took the earl's arm. "So far so good," she murmured.

"So far," he repeated gloomily.

She sent him a surprised look. "I thought we did quite well in the carriage." She smiled at him. "Now, if you can only do as well with Psyche."

That, he thought, was the tricky part.

Gresham joined them outside the door to the

213

inn. "She's all right," he said to Overton. "He's got her locked in a room upstairs."

"Who?" Overton demanded, frowning fiercely. "Who did this dastardly thing?"

"I don't know him," Gresham said, herding him in. "I couldn't see his face. Come, it's this way."

He led them up the narrow stairs. "There, that door."

Overton squared his shoulders, thrust out his chin, and threw himself against the door. Fortunately it was an old door with weakened hinges. When he hit it, it gave way immediately and he burst into the room, the earl right on his heels.

Amanda cowered on the cot, rumpled and disheveled. As they burst through the door, she raised a teary face and sobbed, "Oh, Phillip, I knew you'd come!"

A little melodramatic, the earl thought, but otherwise quite effective. Overton certainly seemed impressed. He gave vent to a string of curses unfit for female ears, rushed across the room, and pulled her into his arms. "Where is the scoundrel?" he demanded angrily. "Has he hurt you? I'll kill him!"

"No, no," Amanda mumbled against his waistcoat. "I am fine, only frightened."

Overton held her off from him, scrutinizing her face. "You're quite sure? You're not just saying that?"

"I'm quite sure," Amanda repeated, clutching at him again.

"Thank goodness!" Overton looked around as though he expected the villain to be waiting for him. "Now, where is that scoundrel? I'm going to beat him within an inch of his miserable—"

"He's gone," Amanda said quickly. "I think he knew he'd been found out. Anyway, he ran off." She sobbed against him. "Oh, Phillip, thank goodness you're here! I was so terribly frightened."

The earl watched this little scene with some amusement. Amanda was better versed in womanly wiles than he had supposed. In fact, she was almost expert. But she could not have learned of these tricks from Psyche. Psyche knew nothing of any modes of female deception—or if she did, she refused to use them.

Overton again held Amanda at arm's length. "I must talk to you seriously," he began, his voice stern.

Amanda's lower lip quivered. "Of course, Phillip."

"You have been turning down all your suitors. Each and every one."

A single tear slipped from her eye, slid slowly down her cheek. "Yes, Phillip."

"I want you to marry. You know that."

"But—"

"And so I have chosen a husband for you."

The girl looked positively stricken. "You— You have?"

"Yes. And I want you to think most seriously about this."

215

Amanda sniffled. "Ye— Yes, Phillip."

Overton frowned, looking grim. "Now, the men who've asked for you have not been to your liking. You didn't care for them. Am I right about this?"

"Yes, Phillip."

"You didn't know them and you were fearful. But you know this man I have in mind. So there's no need to fear. You know him well."

Amanda's lip trembled even more. "I—I do?"

"Yes!" Overton shouted. "It's me! I want you to marry *me!*"

"Oh, yes!" Amanda cried, throwing herself into his arms with such force that she nearly took them both to the floor. "Oh, yes, Phillip! I want to marry you!"

As his friend folded Amanda into his arms, the earl turned away. There in the corridor stood Georgie and Gresham, staring into each other's eyes like a couple of lovesick calves. Another couple in love.

He sighed. Where was Psyche? He couldn't put this off any longer.

Catching Gresham's eye, he mouthed her name.

Gresham pointed to the next door and grinned.

The earl approached the room with some trepidation. He wanted to ask her, he had to ask her, and yet he was afraid. He knocked. There was no answer. He knocked again.

The door opened. Psyche stood there, staring up at him, her eyes questioning. "Did it—"

"Overton just proposed to Amanda. And of

course she accepted. Our mission is accomplished."

Psyche nodded. "That's wonderful." She turned away, back into the room so he couldn't see her face. She didn't feel wonderful, she felt just awful. Now that she had no more reason to remain in London, no more reason to be with the earl, she wasn't sure she could bear to leave.

"So," he said, stepping into the room after her. "Lady Bluestocking has won again. But this time no one will know."

Psyche nodded, barely keeping the tears in check. No matter how hard she tried, and she had tried hard, she could not escape the past. She turned, swallowing hastily. "My—work here is done. It's time for me to return to Sussex."

The earl nodded, his face grave. "Yes, I suppose your steward will need instruction. But don't you think that first you should lay Lady Bluestocking to rest?"

She stared at him for long moments. "I should like to," she said finally. "But I don't know how."

The earl smiled, a strange smile. Even in her sadness she noticed its strangeness.

"Perhaps I can help you," he said.

"I don't see how."

He nodded. "Well, when you attend Amanda's wedding—and then Georgie's—"

Psyche barely kept herself from crying out. So Georgie had won him after all. Vivacious, chattering, empty-headed Georgie had won the most wonderful man in the world.

217

"If you attend these weddings" he went on, "everyone will see that you are not against matrimony."

Psyche nodded, but she hardly heard what he was saying. Georgie could have any man in London. Why did she have to have the earl? Psyche looked down, clenching her hands into fists, hiding them in her skirts. She grit her teeth; she would not cry.

"But I know an even better way," he continued, his tone conversational.

She raised her eyes in surprise. "Better? How?"

"You can get married yourself. Certainly that would put an end to any and all talk."

She couldn't see him clearly through the tears that filmed her eyes. She swallowed hard, trying to laugh, trying to come up with some joking comment. But no words would come. She could do nothing but stare up into his eyes.

He made a peculiar, almost tortured, sound. "I suppose this means you're refusing me?"

Refusing him? What did he mean? Her heart rose up in her throat and her tongue refused to work properly.

"I am asking you to marry me," the earl said ruefully. "But it appears I have made a mistake."

She heard him. He *had* said it! But— She finally found her tongue. "I thought— You said— Aren't you marrying Georgie?"

"Georgie! Good Lord, no!" He looked shocked. "She's out there in the hall with Gresham. They mean to marry each other."

"But— But—" Psyche was feeling dreadfully confused. "Georgie said she wanted you. She hung on you. She flirted with you. She—"

"She was helping me," the earl said heavily. "She told me that jealousy was the way to get you. But obviously she was wrong." He took a tentative step toward her. "I am sorry, Psyche. I— I hope we can remain friends."

"But why—" she asked. "Why didn't you tell *me* you loved me?"

"You're Lady Bluestocking. I—I didn't know how to approach you. So I talked Overton into getting you to manage Amanda's come-out." He sighed. "Oh, he didn't know it was my idea. Remember, I told you that being subtle works best with him."

She stared at him. "But why—why love me?"

"When I was in Spain," he said. "My mother wrote me often. And since she wished to make her letters entertaining, she told me about Lady Bluestocking's arrival in town, all the latest *on-dits,* and the shocks the lady delivered to the ton."

She was trying to take this all in. He read bewilderment in her eyes. "But—" she began.

Maybe he still had a chance! "I know it sounds strange," he continued, afraid to pause, afraid to give her an opportunity to say a definite no. "But you became real to me, more real than the carnage and pain around me. I made a picture of you in my mind. Envisioned you from the details my mother provided."

He wished he knew what to say, how to reach her. She looked so shocked, so dazed. "I know this is a surprise to you, but please don't let it spoil our friendship."

Why did she stare at him like that, her eyes so wide, so bright with tears? Damnation! "I'm sorry if I offended you," he went on softly. "But I truly think we could deal together quite well. And I have loved you for such a long time."

"Loved?" Psyche muttered, looking even more bewildered.

Why hadn't he kept his mouth shut, why had he been in such a rush to spoil things between them? What if she would no longer even allow him friendship?"

He took her hand in his. She was trembling and his legs weren't in much better case. "Psyche, please. Don't send me away."

Her pansy eyes widened. "Send you away," she repeated.

His heart sank down to his boots. She couldn't— He'd been so patient, waited so long. He pulled her into his arms, her body warm against his. "Psyche," he murmured into her hair. "Psyche, I love you. I need you. Please, please, love me. Marry me."

She leaned back in his arms, her eyes glittering with tears. Her lips trembled. He could contain himself no longer. Bending, he kissed her. Gathering her to him in an almost frantic embrace, he poured into his kiss all the love and longing of those lonely months of waiting.

It seemed to him that she responded, but his heart was pounding so that he could hardly breathe. And in the condition he was in he didn't know how to gauge anything. Finally he released her mouth, looking down into her eyes. "Psyche, for God's sake say *something.*"

Psyche moistened her lips. He loved her! He really loved her! The wonder of it was almost more than she could bear. "Yes," she whispered.

He stood there, staring.

"Yes," she repeated, her voice stronger. "I will marry you, though it took you forever to ask me. But you must promise me one thing!"

"Anything, love," he promised, smiling at her with such joy that she thought her heart would overflow. "What is it?"

She searched his face earnestly. "You must promise not to throw my Lady Bluestocking sentiments up to me. I should like to forget all about her."

He nodded. "I promise." He pulled her closer. "But I don't really want to forget Lady Bluestocking. She brought us together and—"

"Here you are!" cried Georgie, popping around the corner from the hall and pulling Gresham after her. She looked them over, observing that Psyche stood in the circle of the earl's arms. Georgie grinned. "Does this mean—"

Psyche laughed. "It means that we are going to be married," Psyche said. "And I hear—"

"Yes," Georgie said, leaning possessively against Gresham's shoulder. "Gresham asked and

I said yes. He's a good man and I've loved him for a long time."

"Say!" Overton came into the room, Amanda clinging to his arm. "What's going on here?" he demanded, his face darkening.

"It's very simple," Amanda explained, sending Psyche a smile. "The earl and Psyche are in love. They're going to get married."

Overton frowned in bewilderment. "But how did Psyche get *here?*"

Amanda smiled up at him and patted his sleeve. "It's a long story, Phillip, dear. A Lady Bluestocking story. Come, I'll tell it to you on the way home."

THE ROMANCES OF LORDS AND LADIES
IN JANIS LADEN'S REGENCIES

BEWITCHING MINX   (2532, $3.95)

From her first encounter with the Marquis of Penderleigh when he had mistaken her for a common trollop, Penelope had been incensed with the darkly handsome lord. Miss Penelope Larchmont was undoubtedly the most outspoken young lady Penderleigh had ever known, and the most tempting.

A NOBLE MISTRESS   (2169, $3.95)

Moriah Landon had always been a singularly practical young lady. So when her father lost the family estate over a game of picquet, she paid the winner, the notorious Viscount Roane, a visit. And when he suggested the means of payment—that she become Roane's mistress—she agreed without a blink of her eyes.

SAPPHIRE TEMPTATION   (3054, $3.95)

Lady Serena was commonly held to be an unusual young girl—outspoken when she should have been reticent, lively when she should have been demure. But there was one tradition she had not been allowed to break: a Wexley must marry a Gower. Richard Gower intended to teach his wife her duties—in every way.

SCOTTISH ROSE   (2750, $3.95)

The Duke of Milburne returned to Milburne Hall trusting that the new governess, Miss Rose Beacham, had instilled the fear of God into his harum-scarum brood of siblings. But she romped with the children, refused to be cowed by his stern admonitions, and was so pretty that he had the devil of a time keeping his hands off her.

FEEL THE FIRE IN CAROL FINCH'S ROMANCES!

BELOVED BETRAYAL (2346, $3.95)

Sabrina Spencer donned a gray wig and veiled hat before blackmailing rugged Ridge Tanner into guiding her to Fort Canby. But the costume soon became her prison—the beauty had fallen head over heels in love!

LOVE'S HIDDEN TREASURE (2980, $4.50)

Shandra d'Evereux felt her heart throb beneath the stolen map she'd hidden in her bodice when Nolan Elliot swept her out onto the veranda. It was hard to concentrate on her mission with that wily rogue around!

MONTANA MOONFIRE (3263, $4.95)

Just as debutante Victoria Flemming-Cassidy was about to marry an oh-so-suitable mate, the towering preacher, Dru Sullivan flung her over his shoulder and headed West! Suddenly, Tori realized she had been given the best present for a bride: a night of passion with a real man!

THUNDER'S TENDER TOUCH (2809, $4.50)

Refined Piper Malone needed bounty-hunter, Vince Logan to recover her swindled inheritance. She thought she could coolly dismiss him after he did the job, but she never counted on the hot flood of desire she felt whenever he was near!